"Just like old times."

"Not in the slightest."

"Be patient," Ross said softly. "You'll be surprised how easy it will be to turn the clock back."

"You're wrong," Macy said. "Everything's changed. I'm not the same trusting, gullible fool I was when we first met...."

SARA CRAVEN was born in south Devon, England, and grew up surrounded by books, in a house by the sea. After leaving grammar school she worked as a local journalist, covering everything from flower shows to murders. She started writing for Harlequin in 1976. Apart from writing, her passions include films, music, cooking and eating in good restaurants. She has two children and now lives in Somerset.

Books by Sara Craven

Sara Craven

Thunder on the Reef

Harlequin Books

TORONTO • NEW YORK • LONDON
AMSTERDAM • PARIS • SYDNEY • HAMBURG
STOCKHOLM • ATHENS • TOKYO • MILAN
MADRID • WARSAW • BUDAPEST • AUCKLAND

ISBN 0-373-11761-2

THUNDER ON THE REEF

First North American Publication 1995.

Copyright © 1994 by Sara Craven.

CHAPTER ONE

SHE knew, of course, that she was being watched.

In normal circumstances, it wouldn't have bothered her too much. She was accustomed, even hardened, to the effect her spectacular looks had on people. She'd even learned to live with the flash of cameras when she appeared in public, and the resulting pictures in glossy magazines. 'Sir Edwin Gilmour's lovely daughter.'

Macy's mouth curled in self-derision. At one time that had seemed the only identity she possessed. But not any more. She was someone in her own right now, with a life—a career that had been almost a salvation.

And that was why she was here on Fortuna— to prove to Cameron and her father and the rest of the board at Gilmour-Denys that the nursery slopes of property negotiation were behind her, and she could handle deals even as tricky as the purchase of Thunder Cay promised to be.

And the last thing she needed was to be recognised at this stage in the game, she thought with irritation as she sipped her iced tea, and tried to ignore the prolonged and intense scrutiny she could feel being directed at her from the other side of Fortuna Town's bustling Main Street.

Because any negotiations for Thunder Cay were to be strictly confidential. The unexpected tip-off Sir Edwin had received had made that clear. Any hint that the island might be on the market would bring other types of shark to those normally inhabiting Bahamian waters thronging around.

'And we have to be first,' he'd said with intensity. 'Our syndicate wants that land, and I— I need this deal, Macy.' For a moment there was a note of something like desperation in his voice. She'd stiffened in alarm, her eyes searching his face, questions teeming in her brain, but, after a moment, he'd continued more calmly, 'I'd go myself, of course, but if I was spotted it would give the game away immediately. So it's all down to you, my dear.'

She'd said, 'No problem,' with more confidence than she actually possessed.

The elaborate model for the hotel and leisure complex which would turn Thunder Cay into the Bahamas' latest and most expensive resort had graced the penthouse office at Gilmour-Denys for a long time now.

Privately, Macy had termed it the Impossible Dream, because Boniface Hilliard, the reclusive millionaire who owned Thunder Cay, had always adamantly refused to sell. She'd been convinced he never would.

Yet in the last week, a whisper had reached Edwin Gilmour's ears from some grapevine that the old man, a childless widower, was said to be ill, and prepared to discuss the disposal of some of his assets.

Thunder Cay wouldn't be the only item up for grabs, Macy thought. There was the fortune he'd made from investment worldwide, and the mansion Trade Winds, overlooking the best beach on the south side of Fortuna itself.

But the bulk of his massive estate wasn't her concern. All she had to do was convince his lawyer, Mr Ambrose Delancey, to recommend Gilmour-Denys's bid for Thunder Cay to his client. For someone apparently prepared to negotiate, Mr Delancey had proved annoyingly elusive. She'd spent three fruitless days so far, trying to make an appointment with him.

Ostensibly, of course, she was a tourist, booked into Fortuna's main hotel, using her mother's maiden name Landin as an added precaution. She'd thought she'd be safe enough. Fortuna, after all, wasn't one of the most fashionable islands of the Bahamas. It didn't appeal to the jet-setters and generally well-heeled who thronged to New Providence and Paradise Islands, and there were no *paparazzi* eagerly face-spotting around the bars and cafes on Main Street, or the bustling harbour area.

On the whole, it was a man's resort, a haven for the big-game fishermen who came to chase the bluefin tuna, the sailfish and the blue marlin by day, and enjoy a nightlife more lively than sophisticated when darkness fell.

Accordingly, Macy had deliberately played down her appearance, choosing a plain navy shift dress, with matching low-heeled leather sandals, as well as concealing her cloud of mahogany-coloured hair under a bandanna, and masking her slanting green eyes behind an oversized pair of sunglasses.

And yet, incredibly, it seemed she'd still been recognised. Damn and blast it, she thought with exasperation.

She ventured a swift, sideways glance across the busy road, searching between the slow-moving hurly burly of carts, street-vendors' bicycles, and luridly hued taxis.

She saw him at once, lounging against an ancient pick-up, its rust spots held together by a virulent yellow paint-job. He was tall, with a shaggy mane of curling dark hair, the upper part of his face concealed behind sunglasses as un-revealing as her own, the lower hidden by de-signer stubble. But even from a distance she could see his teeth gleam in a smile of totally cynical appraisal.

The rest of him, Macy noted, bristling at the implications of that unashamed grin, was bronze skin interrupted by a sleeveless denim waist-coat, and matching trousers raggedly cut off at mid-thigh.

He was as disreputable as his tatty vehicle, she thought with contempt, averting her gaze. A later-day Bahamian pirate turned beach-bum. She supposed that, as a woman sitting alone at a pavement table, she was obvious prey for his kind. Nevertheless that prolonged, oddly intense observation made her feel uneasy—restless, almost unnerved.

Idiot, she thought, glancing at her watch, then signalling to the waiter, as she finished her tea. She was out of here anyway. It was time to find her way to the office of Ambrose Delancey, attorney-at-law.

As the bill was placed in front of her, a shadow fell across the table. A tanned hand dropped a scatter of loose change on to the folded slip in the saucer.

And a voice she'd never thought to hear again said laconically, 'Have this on me, Macy.'

Shock mingled with disbelief paralysed her. Turned her dumb. The traffic noises, and the buzz of laughter and chatter around her faded into dizzying silence. All she could hear, echoing and re-echoing in her brain, were those few drawled words.

Turning her ordered world to sudden reeling chaos.

Her nails became claws, curling into the palms of her hands, scoring the soft flesh. But, as they did so, bringing her back to stark reality.

No wonder, she thought, swallowing back sudden nausea. No wonder she'd felt uneasy. Some undreamed of sixth sense must have been warning her.

She turned her head slowly. Looked up, with an assumption of calm enquiry.

He was standing over her, close enough to touch. She had to force herself not to shrink away. But it was imperative not to allow him any kind of ascendancy.

She said coolly, 'Ross. What a surprise.'

'You could say that.' He sounded faintly amused, as he hitched a chair forward. 'Mind if I join you?'

His presumption galled her. She said between her teeth, 'Yes, I bloody well do mind,' and he laughed.

'Now that's far more in character.' He looked her over, a tingling top to toe assessment that missed nothing on the way, and made her cringe inside with anger, and a kind of unwilling excitement. 'You're looking good.'

'I wish I could say the same for you,' she said tersely. 'I didn't recognise you.'

'Now I,' he said softly, 'would have known you anywhere. The beautiful Macy Gilmour. I hope I've got the label right.'

'Absolutely.' She pushed the coins back at him. 'Save these for your next meal.'

'Always the soul of generosity.'

'A family trait,' she said. 'But maybe you don't remember.'

'By no means. I recall all the details of every transaction between us, Macy, my sweet, sexual as well as financial.' His voice lingered on the words, deliberately creating all kinds of intimate images. Deliberately winding her up, she realised with vexation, feeling swift blood rise unbidden in her face,

'Fortunately, I don't,' she said crisply, trying to take control of herself, and the situation. She couldn't believe what was happening to her. For four years, she'd striven to dismiss Ross Bannister from her mind as completely as he'd disappeared from her life. Of all the people in the world, she thought despairingly. Of all the places in the world. And of all the lousy, stinking, rotten luck.

'So, what brings you to Fortuna?' Ross asked lazily, sitting down in spite of her denial.

'I'm on holiday,' she returned shortly. To her annoyance, the waiter whisked away the bill and the money before she could stop him, lifting a hand to Ross in obvious camaraderie as he did so.

Above the enigmatic shades, his brows lifted sardonically. 'Are all the usual flesh pots fully booked? I wouldn't have thought this was your scene, although there are some good beaches.' He paused. 'I won't tell you to watch out for sharks. You've been mixing with them all your life.'

'You,' she said, 'were the first.' She reached for her bag, and got to her feet.

'Going so soon?' Ross rose too, with a courtesy so exaggerated it bordered on insolence. 'But our reunion has hardly begun.'

'Wrong,' she said. Her mouth was dry, her heart was hammering. 'It never started.'

He stroked his chin meditatively. 'I hope the beard hasn't put you off.'

'By no means,' she returned. 'It looks wholly appropriate. Wasn't there a pirate called Blackbeard?'

'Indeed there was,' he said. 'He used to operate round Nassau way.'

'What a pity you don't do the same.'

'I prefer to work on a smaller scale.' She'd forgotten his smile. Forgotten too how heart-stoppingly handsome he was, in spite of the scruffy hair and stubble. In fact, there was a lot about Ross Bannister she'd have preferred to dismiss permanently from her mind.

'You're not very relaxed for a holidaymaker,' he commented. 'You seem constantly on edge.'

'Do you wonder?' She paused. 'May I be frank?'

'You always were,' he murmured.

'Thank you.' She faced him squarely, chin up. 'The fact is, Ross, I'd hoped you were out of my life forever. Meeting you again is like the worst kind of bad dream.'

'Well, that is being frank. Unfortunately for you, it could also be a recurring dream,' he said. 'This is only a small island. We could bump into each other quite regularly.'

'No.' She said it so loudly and vehemently that people at neighbouring tables looked at them curiously.

'Alternatively,' Ross went on imperturbably, 'you could always ask your hotel for a transfer to another island.'

If the choice were hers, that was exactly what she'd be doing, Macy thought angrily. Only she couldn't cut and run. Not yet. She had business to attend to. An important deal to get off the ground. Her personal emotions couldn't be allowed to interfere with that.

She said coolly, 'Using the excuse that I'd been frightened by a rat, I suppose. But, no, I don't think so. I like it here.' She paused. 'How much, this time, Ross, to get you out of my life?'

He said softly, 'Forget it, Macy. There wouldn't be room for all the noughts on the cheque.' He slanted a brief smile at her. 'See you around,' he added, and walked away.

Macy walked too, back up the street, oblivious to the jostling of other pedestrians, as she stared unseeingly ahead of her. Her head was whirling, her thoughts going crazy.

It had been four long years since Ross Bannister had walked out on her. Four years in which to heal herself, and rebuild her shattered self-esteem. Find a new identity.

She thought she'd succeeded. But his sudden reappearance, just when she needed it least, had shaken her world to its foundations.

For the first time, she realised just how much her hard-won security and confidence depended on never being reminded of Ross. Certainly of never seeing him again.

Yet, like some evil genius, here he was.

Under the laws of probability, she wondered just what the chances were of them bumping into each other like this. Probably a million to one. It had to be the most appalling coincidence of the decade.

She cursed herself silently for not staying safely in the confines of the hotel until it was time to go to Mr Delancey's office. If she hadn't taken time out to explore, shop-gaze and have a drink at that particular pavement bar, Ross might never have seen her.

She was surprised that he'd recognised her at all. She wasn't the girl he'd left behind four years before. And she was astonished that, after all that had passed between them, he should want to make contact with her again, however fleetingly.

He could have no conscience, she thought bitterly. No sense of shame.

And there was no guarantee this was the only time they'd run into each other.

'This is only a small island...'

Had she imagined the note of warning in his voice? She didn't think so.

She felt sick again. She could always call her father and ask his advice. Except that she knew what he'd say. He'd summon her back instantly, and hand the Thunder Cay negotiations to someone else.

And she didn't want that. She'd fought hard for her place on the Gilmour-Denys team. At first work had been a form of therapy in the wake of Ross's desertion. Lately, she'd become involved for the sake of the job itself.

Among other things, she'd taken over the administration of the charitable trusts left by her wealthy American mother. The bulk of Kathryn Landin's considerable estate, bequeathed to Macy personally, would come to her in four years' time, on her twenty-fifth birthday.

Up to now, her father had acted as her trustee and adviser, while she'd merely been a figurehead, following his direction. She'd gathered, wryly, that that was how he thought matters should continue.

But she had other ideas. She planned to manage the Landin bequest herself, alongside her career at Gilmour-Denys. She had no intention of being treated as a pretty ornament, to be produced at dinner parties and other social events. She had a sharp business acumen like her mother's before her, and no emotional shock, however acute, was going to throw her off balance. She couldn't afford to get hysterical just because an ex-lover had crossed her path.

But not just an ex-lover, said a sly voice in her head. Ross was your first, and only lover. The one you fell so hard for that you gave him your whole life.

Only that wasn't what Ross wanted at all, she thought, inner pain slashing at her. He'd had very different plans for the future.

Don't look back, she adjured herself. Look forward. Concentrate on the job in hand. Make the deal, and get out as fast as you can. The fact that you've seen him doesn't have to affect your plans at all.

As she turned to hail a passing taxi, painted like a mauve and white zebra, she found the image of Ross, tanned and unkempt in his raggy denims, disturbingly entrenched in her mind. Looking, she thought, exactly like the drifter and layabout her father had accused him of being.

She supposed she should be glad her father had been right about him all along. At the same time, she couldn't help wondering exactly what Ross had done with all that money.

The money her father had paid him to get out of her life forever.

Ambrose Delancey's law offices were situated on the first floor of a pleasant white-painted building, in a square of similar buildings.

In the middle of the square was a fountain, surrounded by flower-beds, and surmounted by a statue of a man dressed in the elaborate style of the seventeenth century. A plaque announced that this was Bevis Hilliard, Fortuna's first governor.

As a family, the Hilliards had clearly enjoyed power here from the first. The sale of Thunder Cay was the first chink in the wall of autocracy they'd built around themselves. A tacit acknowledgement, perhaps, that Boniface Hilliard was the last of his name.

There was a certain sadness about that, Macy thought, as she went into the office building.

She found herself in a small reception area, confronted by a girl with a smile as wide as the sky.

'My name's Landin,' she introduced herself. 'And I have an appointment with Mr Delancey.'

'He's expecting you, Miz Landin.' The girl lifted a phone and spoke softly into it. 'Will you take a seat for just one minute. May I get you some coffee, or a cold drink?'

Macy declined politely. She was feeling frankly nervous, and took several deep breaths to restore her equilibrium.

Then a buzzer sounded sharply, and she was shown through a door at the rear of the room into a large office. One wall was mostly window, shielded against the worst of the sun by slatted blinds. Two of the other walls were lined in books, and a display of green plants gave an impression of coolness as well as discreetly masking another door, presumably leading to further offices.

Ambrose Delancey was a tall black man, impeccably clad in a lightweight cream suit. He greeted Macy with reserved friendliness and a firm handshake.

'What can I do for you, Miss Landin?' he asked, offering her a black leather chair in front of his imposing desk.

'I hope you can open negotiations for the sale of Thunder Cay to Gilmour-Denys,' Macy returned coolly and crisply. 'You've seen a copy of our proposal, and had time to consider it. We'd now like to hear your client's response.'

Mr Delancey smiled reluctantly. 'You don't waste any time. But this is Fortuna, Miss Landin, and we take things at a slower pace here.'

'So I've noticed,' Macy said drily.

'I'm not saying my client isn't interested in your offer,' Mr Delancey went on. 'But there are certain—formalities he insists on, before any serious discussion takes place.'

'What kind of formalities?'

He toyed absently with a pen. 'The fact is, Miss Landin, Mr Hilliard wishes to meet you.'

'To meet me?' Macy was taken aback. 'Why should he want that—at this stage?'

He shrugged. 'Maybe he wants to assess the calibre of your company from you as its representative.' He let that sink in, then continued, 'I take it you have no objection?'

'No,' she said. 'If that's what it takes. Will you arrange a further meeting here?'

He shook his head. 'Mr Hilliard's state of health doesn't permit that, so the interview will be at Trade Winds. I'll contact you at your hotel as soon as the appointment's been made. I trust that's convenient.'

'Perfectly,' Macy returned. It seemed to her that Mr Delancey's gaze had strayed a couple of times towards the door in the corner, and that she'd heard vague sounds of movement from behind it. Another client, she surmised, growing restive.

She got to her feet. 'I realise how busy you are,' she said pointedly. 'I'll wait to hear from you.'

Outside, in the baking afternoon heat, she drew a deep, shaky breath. What did they say about the best laid plans?

It seemed that, for good or ill, she was stuck here indefinitely.

She would have to wait with as much patience as she could muster for her summons to Trade Winds. Play the game on Fortuna terms. She wasn't enamoured of the idea of being inspected by Boniface Hilliard, but there was no point in objecting. Softly, softly was the only approach.

Under different circumstances, of course, she could have shrugged off the inconvenience, even enjoyed her enforced break, especially as this was her first time in the Bahamas.

If, that was, it weren't for Ross...

His presence on Fortuna made all the difference, of course. That was why she was so on edge, she thought.

'This is only a small island.' That was what he'd said. And 'See you around.'

Macy tasted blood suddenly, and realised she had sunk her teeth deep into her bottom lip.

'Not,' she said under her breath, staring up at the merciless blue of the sky, 'not if I see him first.'

CHAPTER TWO

MACY still felt restive as she showered and changed for dinner that evening.

She put on white silk trousers and a matching sleeveless, low-necked top, defining her slender waist with a favourite belt of broad silver links. Her hair she pinned up into a loose coil, and she hung silver hoops in her ears.

She looked like the ideal tourist, anticipating an evening of leisure and pleasure, she thought, grimacing at her reflection before turning away.

She'd spent a quiet afternoon in a sheltered corner of the hotel gardens, making herself think coolly and rationally about the best course to follow when she came face to face with Boniface Hilliard. How to make the best impression.

But in spite of everything, her thoughts kept turning compulsively back to Ross, although she knew she was a fool and worse than a fool to let him impinge even marginally on her consciousness.

She didn't mention his presence when she left a message on her father's answering machine about the latest development in the negotiations.

What Sir Edwin didn't know wouldn't hurt him, she told herself defensively. She could imagine only too well how he'd react if he discovered Ross was within a thousand miles of her again.

But then they'd been oil and water from their first meeting, she recalled with an inward shudder. On almost every issue—personal, professional, and political—they'd been on opposite sides of a steadily widening gulf, with her, trapped between them, suspended over some bitter, bottomless pit of divided loyalties.

But she'd still hoped, with absurd optimism, that they might learn to get along for her sake.

But then I was very naïve in those days, she thought in self-derision. My father, of course, saw through Ross right away—realised he was simply on the make. Why couldn't I have believed him instead of finding out the hard way?

In the thatched roof bar, adjoining the hotel dining-room, she chose a table overlooking the sea, and ordered a Margarita while she studied the menu.

Once again she knew she was the object of scrutiny, but this time no mental alarms were being sounded. She was simply encountering the usual speculative, semi-lustful attention that women on their own tended to be subjected to. And apart from closeting herself in her bungalow, or wearing a bag over her head, there wasn't a great deal she could do except ignore it, and hope the hint would be taken.

The menu was heavily weighted towards seafood. Macy had noticed the huge conch shell displayed at the dining-room entrance, and conch was being offered cracked, frittered, as a salad or in the ever-popular chowder, along with grouper, snapper, and stewfish.

I wish I were going to be here to sample them all, she thought, wondering at the same time how long she was going to be kept dangling.

After due deliberation, she decided on asparagus tips in chive butter, baked in a pastry case, followed by lobster tails grilled with garlic and lemon juice, and accompanied by a bottle of crisp white wine.

As the waiter left, Macy realised uncomfortably that there'd been no relaxation in the attention she was attracting. In particular, she was being fixedly stared at by an overweight man with thinning red hair and the loudest sports shirt in the Western hemisphere, who was sitting at the bar with three male companions of similar age and build.

Macy delved into her bag and produced a paperback novel, using it as a barrier as she sipped her drink. Usually it worked. But not always, apparently.

An ingratiating voice said, 'All on your own, sweetheart.'

The colours in his shirt were even more dazzling close at hand.

'Yes.' Macy kept her voice cool and level. 'And that's how I prefer it, thanks.'

'Aw, come on, be friendly.' The man put another Margarita down in front of her, then deposited himself in the opposite chair with his own beer. 'Strangers in a foreign land, and all that.'

Macy's lips tightened. She said quietly, with glacial emphasis, 'Would you rejoin your friends, please? I didn't ask you to join me, and I don't want another drink.'

'I'm under orders to bring you back with me,' her unwanted companion said with a leer. 'We'd like to buy you dinner, a few drinks, a few laughs—know what I mean?'

Only too well, she thought, her heart sinking.

Aloud, she said, 'You're beginning to annoy me. Would you please leave me alone?'

'What's the matter. Think we can't afford you?' He showed her a wallet, stuffed to the gills with Bahamian dollars.

'Very impressive.' Macy lifted her chin. 'Now go away before I call the manager.'

He snorted. 'Call who you like, girlie, and let them draw their own conclusions. Lookers like you don't hang around on their own in bars for no reason.'

'But the lady's not by herself.' Another voice, icily incisive, and all-too-familiar, cut into the confrontation. 'She's with me, and we'd both like you to leave.'

Macy's lips parted in a gasp of astonished outrage as Ross bent, lightly brushing his lips across her cheek.

'I'm sorry I'm late.' His eyes smiled into hers, challenging her to deny him. 'Has it caused problems?'

'Nothing I couldn't handle,' she returned tautly, glaring back at him. This time her warning antennae had let her down badly.

'So I noticed.' He turned to Loud Shirt who was already making himself scarce, apologising volubly for any misunderstanding.

Ross watched him go, hands on hips, then turned back to Macy, who was struggling to regain her self-command. She could still feel the brief touch of his lips on her face as if she'd been branded there.

How dared he take advantage of the situation like that? she thought angrily. But she couldn't tax him with it. The last thing she wanted Ross to know was that he still had the power to disturb her. Play it cool, she adjured herself, her stomach churning.

He was hardly recognisable as the man who'd accosted her that morning, she realised dazedly. The stubble had gone, his hair had been trimmed slightly, and instead of ragged denims he was wearing faultlessly cut grey trousers, fitting closely to his long legs, and a short sleeved, open-necked shirt, striped in charcoal and white. There was a thin platinum watch on his left wrist, too.

He looked a combination of toughness and affluence.

Ross turned back to her. 'You shouldn't have any more trouble there,' he said.

'No,' she acknowledged stiffly, adding a reluctant, 'Thank you.'

His grin was sardonic. 'I bet that hurt.'

She ignored that. 'What are you doing here?'

'This is a good restaurant. I like to eat.'

'Oh.' There was no real answer to that, she thought, nonplussed.

'Also,' he went on softly. 'We have some unfinished business to conduct.' He pulled up a chair and sat down, signalling the waiter to bring him a Bourbon and water.

Macy's heart began to thud apprehensively. She said, 'Rather an expensive place to do business, surely.'

'Oh, I've been able to afford something better than hamburger joints for some time.' The cool aquamarine gaze flickered over her, lingering openly and shamelessly on the thrust of her breasts against the white silk top.

Macey felt the breath catch in her throat, and the tremor of an almost forgotten weakness invade her stomach. She struggled to keep her voice level. 'Of course. I was forgetting.'

'No, darling,' he said gently. 'You haven't forgotten a thing, and neither, I promise you, have I.'

Her uneasiness increased, and she was thankful to see the waiter approaching.

'Your table's ready, Miz Landin.' He turned to her companion. 'How yo' doin', Mister Ross. You dinin' here tonight?'

'Yes, with Miss—er—Landin here.' Ross's oblique glance dared her to object. 'Just a steak, George, please. Medium rare with a side salad.'

When George had gone, Macy said thickly, 'You have one hell of a nerve.'

'Since childhood,' he agreed. 'But as I told your would-be admirer we were together, we can hardly eat in isolation.' He paused. 'Unless you'd prefer to join his party, after all. They look like a fun-loving bunch.'

Macy gave him a fulminating glance, and stalked ahead of him into the restaurant.

Their table, to her annoyance, was in a secluded corner, lit by a small lamp under a pretty glass shade. The centrepiece was orchids, cream edged with flame, swimming in a shallow bowl. Macy sat down, her lips compressed at the overt romanticism of it all, aware, also, of the resentful gaze of Loud Shirt and his friends a few tables away.

At least she'd been spared any further harassment from that quarter, she thought, but at what cost to her own peace of mind? Instead she had to dine with a man who'd rejected her love, and whose mercenary heartlessness was almost beyond belief.

'So, why Miss Landin?' Ross asked, as he took his seat. 'Are you travelling incognito for some reason?'

Macy gave a shrug, trying to sound casual. 'Not particularly. I like to use my mother's name sometimes.'

'I'm sure you do.' There was an odd note in his voice which she found it impossible to decipher. But that was the least of her problems, she thought grimly.

Her appetite seemed to have deserted her, but to cancel dinner would give Ross some kind of psychological advantage, which she couldn't allow. She had to convince him—and herself too—that his presence was a matter of indifference to her.

So, she'd eat this meal if it choked her. As well it might.

'The chef's name is Clyde,' Ross said, watching her push her first course round her plate. 'He's a sensitive soul, and it'll spoil his night if you send one of his specialities back to the kitchen.'

'Oh.' She gave him a hostile look and dug her fork into the puff pastry crust. To her annoyance, it melted in the mouth, and the asparagus tips were ambrosial.

'I'd say this holiday of yours is long overdue,' he went on. 'You have that indoor look—very unhealthy.'

'As a matter of fact,' she offered curtly, 'I've never felt better in my life.'

'Then you should be extremely worried.' Ross poured the wine. 'For one thing, you're like a cat on hot bricks.'

'Is it really any wonder?' She put down her fork. 'I thought I'd made it clear you're the last person in the world I ever wanted to meet again.'

He lifted his glass in a mock toast. 'I apologise for my inconvenient existence.' He paused, his glance speculative. 'You sound incredibly bitter, Macy. They're not all bad memories, surely.'

'Not for you, perhaps,' she snapped.

'Or for you, my lovely hypocrite.' A reminiscent smile played about the corners of his mouth. 'We had our moments.' He leaned forward, his eyes holding hers across the table. 'Shall I jog your memory?'

'No,' she said hoarsely. 'I don't...'

'That sexy French film we went to see,' he said softly. 'My God, you were so turned on, you practically dragged me back to the flat. We were undressing each other on the way up the stairs.'

'Stop it,' she hissed desperately.

'And then there was that evening at the bistro round the corner,' he went on relentlessly. 'When the guitarist played all your favourite love songs, and a girl came round, selling roses.'

He touched the edge of one of the orchids with the tip of his finger.

She remembered the rose he'd bought her, crimson and long-stemmed. In bed that night he'd teased her nipples with its dusky velvet petals...

Her throat closed.

'Enjoy your trip down memory lane,' she said harshly. 'It does nothing for me.'

'No?' His smiling gaze shifted again to the revealing outline of her breasts. 'You don't seem entirely unmoved, darling.'

'You disgust me.' She pushed her plate away.

'Then I'll try and control my baser urges for the rest of the meal, at least.'

He paused. 'So—why Fortuna, Macy?'

Her heart jumped. She had not, she thought grimly, been expecting that. She swallowed. 'Why not? I've been working very hard. As you say, I needed a break.'

'Perhaps,' he said. 'But unless you're into big-game fishing, the island hasn't a great deal to offer.'

'Oh, I wouldn't say that.' I'm after a different kind of game, she added silently. Mr Boniface Hilliard himself. She shrugged, allowing herself a negligent smile. 'But maybe I'm just easily pleased.'

'No,' he said gently. 'I don't think so.' He sat back giving her a reflective look over the top of his glass. 'You haven't told me yet what you do to earn this arduous crust of yours.'

Macy hesitated. The last thing she wanted was to mention her connection with Gilmour-Denys.

'I'm involved with the Landin Trust now,' she returned neutrally.

'A heavy responsibility, indeed.' His tone was ironic.

'As you, with your fondness for money, would be the first to appreciate,' she bit back, and saw his mouth tighten.

'You've always found cash the answer to everything yourself, my pet. Let's not forget that.' He paused. 'I hope it hasn't been your only means of fulfilment over the past years.'

'By no means,' she said sharply, and he lifted an eyebrow.

'Why, Macy,' he drawled. 'Are you telling me you've been unfaithful?'

'I'm telling you nothing,' she said.

'You're denying my right to know?'

'You have no rights where I'm concerned,' she said. 'Not any more.'

He looked at her bare hands, clenched in front of her on the table. 'You seem to be overlooking one salient fact, darling,' he said. 'Whether we like it or not, you and I are still legally married.'

'That is a mere formality.' Her voice shook. 'Which I intend to dispense with shortly.

Ross was silent for a moment, toying with the stem of his wine glass. Then he said mildly, 'Do I take it you're here to ask me for a divorce?'

'I'm not here to ask you for anything,' she said. 'I don't need to. In another year, I can end our so-called marriage, even without your consent.'

'How convenient,' he said. 'I'm only surprised you didn't set the ball rolling long ago.'

She looked down at the table. 'You forget, I didn't know where to find you.'

'Of course not. But I imagine Daddy's tracker dogs would have managed it without too much trouble.'

Macy moved quickly, restively before she could stop herself, and his voice sharpened. 'Unless, of course, you still haven't told him. My God, Macy, is that it?' His laugh held disbelief. 'You've kept our marriage a secret all this time?'

She said tightly, 'Who wants to make public a serious error of judgement?'

'Touché,' he said drily. 'Clearly your next choice will be based on sound common sense and good fiscal principles. I wonder if I can make an educated guess at his identity.'

'There's no one. I simply want my legal freedom.'

His brows lifted sceptically. 'You mean Daddy hasn't been able to persuade you to make Cameron Denys a happy man at last. You amaze me.'

Macy bit her lip angrily, aware of a faint betraying flush. Cameron's unswerving pursuit of her, with her father's encouragement, had been a bone of contention between them particularly in the last year. 'Don't be snide about my father,' she said curtly. 'He managed to see through you without much difficulty.'

'And I found him equally transparent. Not that it matters. I never gave a damn what he thought of me. The only opinion I cared about was yours.'

For a moment, she was very still.

She said, 'That must be one of the most cynical statements I've ever heard. You—walked out of my life with a golden handshake of one hundred and fifty thousand pounds. That's how much my—opinion mattered. That's how much I was worth to you.'

Ross's mouth twisted. 'It seemed a pre-emptive offer,' he said, 'leaving no room for negotiation. You have to want to be rid of someone very badly to put up that kind of money.'

'Or have a fairly accurate assessment of their level of greed.' She waited for an explosion of anger, but none came.

Ross merely shrugged. 'They say everyone has their price,' he countered. 'Why argue?'

For me, she thought in sudden, swift agony. You could have argued for me—fought for me— told my father to go to hell and take his insulting offer with him.

But you didn't, Ross—you didn't...

Aloud, 'Why indeed?' she said calmly. 'As a matter of interest, would you have gone for less?'

'Probably, in the circumstances.' He sounded almost casual, she realised, pain slashing at her. 'I hope you're not expecting a refund, Macy.'

'Certainly not,' she retorted briskly. 'It was money well spent.'

'I'm glad you think so,' he said evenly, signalling to the hovering George to bring their main courses. 'If they ever have to open you up for surgery, darling, they'll find a bank statement where your heart should be—and showing a credit balance.'

Macy digested that, smarting, while they were being served.

'So—what did you do with your own credit balance?' she asked, once they were alone again. 'Waste it—gamble it away?'

He was silent for a moment. 'I made good use of it,' he said at last.

'To further your career as a photographer?' She despised herself for asking.

'No.'

The flat monosyllable was uninviting, but she persisted. 'Do you still take photographs?'

'Yes, but I'm commissioned these days. Thanks to you, I don't need to pursue the precarious freelance existence your father objected to so strenuously.' He drank some wine. 'I'm obliged to you.'

'Don't be.' Her bitten lip felt raw. 'All the same, I'm glad for you.'

'Are you?' He sounded sceptical. 'Why?'

She put down her fork. 'Because you were good,' she said slowly. 'I always thought you'd be in some wilderness, making a record of it before the bulldozers moved in and spoiled it. Just as—you always planned.'

She'd nearly said 'we', she realised with a pang. Because it had been a mutual and cherished dream, or so she'd thought. One of the many, she reminded herself, that had died when he'd walked out on her.

'How flattering,' he said softly, 'that you do remember some things at least.'

'Not really.' The last lobster tail tasted like poisoned leather. 'Someone who hurt me as you did isn't easy to forget—however hard one may try.'

'And I'm sure one has tried,' he said courteously. His voice hardened. 'Just what the hell did you expect, Macy? That I'd turn down the money? God knows it was an offer no one could refuse. Wasn't that the whole point of it?' He paused. 'Or were you just testing me?'

She shook her head. 'No, it was quite genuine. You'd have been a fool to walk away from it.'

A fool for love, as I was. I trusted you, Ross. Even when my father told me you were for sale, I didn't believe him. Even when I saw the evidence with my own eyes...

'That's what I thought,' he said. His smile didn't reach his eyes, as he ran a hand over his chin. 'When you saw me earlier, you thought I was down-and-out, looking for handouts, didn't you, my sweet? Well, I'm sorry to disappoint you, but I'm doing fine, which is why I'm so glad to be able to buy you dinner tonight. As a small thank-you for showing me the way—giving me my start in life.'

He shrugged. 'As they say, I'd never have managed it without you.'

'Think nothing of it.' The night air was warm, but Macy felt deathly cold.

'And now George is on his way to ask if you want dessert,' Ross went on. 'I recommend the Key lime pie.'

Macy shook her head. 'Nothing more for me,' she said. 'I—I seem to have lost my appetite.'

'Oh, don't say that.' There was mock concern in his voice. 'You have to be able to keep up with Daddy, Cameron and the rest of the carnivores.'

'How dare you say that?' Macy, trembling, pushed her chair back. 'You have no right. You're not fit to—to...'

'Lick their boots?' Ross supplied silkily. 'Quite right. There are whole gangs of far better qualified people hanging round Gilmour-Denys to do just that. But I never thought you'd be one of them, Macy. What a disappointment.'

'Damn you.' She got to her feet, her breasts rising and falling swiftly under the force of her tangled emotions. 'Damn you to hell, Ross Bannister.'

'Too late, darling. You already did that—four years ago.' He rose too, and came round the table to where she stood. He took her by the shoulders, pulling her towards him. For one endless moment, she felt his mouth on hers, without gentleness, without mercy. An act of stark possession.

And somewhere, buried in the depths of her being, she felt a sharp, unbidden flicker of totally shameful response.

Then, just as suddenly, she was free, staring dazedly up into his cool, aquamarine eyes.

He said expressionlessly, 'Goodnight, Macy. I'll be seeing you.'

Shaking, totally oblivious to the interested stares from the adjoining tables, Macy watched him cross the restaurant, pause briefly to scribble his signature on the bill, then disappear out into the night.

CHAPTER THREE

MACY got back to the bungalow somehow. She slammed the door behind her, and stood, panting, her hands pressed against the woodwork as if she was somehow drawing strength from its solidity.

Her mouth felt ravaged. She could make no sense of anything that had happened that evening, but Ross's kiss had burned itself into her consciousness forever.

She felt as if she was crumbling inside, the sane, rational core she'd come to depend on disintegrating. Meltdown.

Don't be a fool, she thought, staring into the darkness. Ross sold you out in the worst possible way. Betrayed you totally. When he went, you had to drag yourself back from the abyss, and learn to live again. You were the one in hell, not him. Never forget that.

He'd actually thanked her for giving him his start in life, she recalled with stark incredulity. The sheer cruelty of it flayed her like a whip.

But that was all she'd ever been to Ross—a meal ticket—a step on the ladder.

Yet during those first dizzy months he'd made her believe she was everything in the world that he wanted. That she was necessary—even essential to him, like the air he breathed. And she'd accepted that precious valuation—gloried in it. Letting herself forget that no one was indispensable.

'A freelance photographer?' She could still hear her father's voice, lifted in outraged astonishment. 'Does that mean he's not in any kind of regular employment?'

'Well, in a way,' Macy had returned defensively. 'He earns fees from newspapers and magazines when he sells them picture spreads.'

'And does that provide him with a living?'

'Yes, because he's good,' Macy had said flatly. 'He's not rich by your standards, perhaps, but he will be one day. He wants to travel.' Her eyes shone. 'He wants to bring the forgotten places of the world to life—remind us all what we have to treasure, before we throw it all away...'

'My dear child.' Sir Edwin had looked pained. 'Where did you meet this—er—freelance?'

'At an exhibition.' Her smile had almost hugged itself. 'I stood back to get a better look at some pictures and trod on his foot. I thought I'd done permanent damage.'

She giggled, remembering her conscience stricken apologies.

'Have I hurt you?'

'Mortally.' His face was solemn. 'But if you had supper with me tonight, it might ease my final hours...'

'Indeed——' Her father's unwontedly grave voice had brought her back to reality. 'I see that I should have insisted on your accompanying me to the States. Then this unfortunate accident might have been prevented.'

Macy had laughed out loud. 'But I didn't want to avoid it,' she'd objected. 'I'm in love with Ross. We're going to be married.'

After a moment, he said, 'Don't be silly, my pet. You only met him—what?—a fortnight ago. You hardly know him.'

Macy bit her lip. 'Daddy, I know him better than I've ever known anyone in my life.' Even you, she thought, but did not say it.

She'd never heard her father's voice so harsh before. 'Are you saying you've been intimate with this man?'

She knew what he meant, of course, but the use of the word in that context puzzled her. Yes, she'd been intimate with Ross, but in so many ways that had nothing to do with the wild, sweet, crazy passion they'd discovered together on the narrow, hard bed in his flat.

Because, to her, intimacy was also cooking meals together in the impossibly cramped kitchenette, sharing a shower, and the small piece of soap that they kept dropping, seeing Ross shave for the first time, or even watching him read, her own book forgotten, as she scanned, with mounting excitement the strongly moulded contours of his face, until he looked up, alerted in turn by her prolonged scrutiny...

'Macy.' Sir Edwin took hold of her by the shoulders, shook her. 'Answer me.'

She pulled free and stepped back, startled by the sudden grey look in his face.

'Yes, he's my lover,' she said quietly. 'And he's going to be my husband.'

'My God,' her father whispered. 'Have you no shame? Is this all your upbringing—your education has taught you? To jump into bed at the first opportunity with some nobody—some ne'er do well?'

'You've no right to say that,' she flared back at him.

'Very well, then. Who are his family? What is his background? These are questions any father is entitled to ask.'

'I don't know.' She shook her head. 'I suggest you ask him yourself.'

'Don't worry,' Sir Edwin said grimly. 'I shall.'

And even after that, I still hoped they might find some common ground for my sake, Macy thought now, pushing herself away from the door, and treading wearily across the living area to her bedroom. Instead, it had been a total disaster from beginning to end.

Because her father had been quite right. Ross was a stranger to her. She'd never really known him at all. And he was still an enigma even now, she thought, shivering, as she put on the lamp beside her bed.

Across the room, reflected in the long mirror, she saw again the image of a girl, dressed in white, pale-faced, her eyes wide with strain, her mouth bruised and swollen from a kiss. A stranger's kiss...

Then, and only then, she burst into tears.

The bed was wide and cool, with the crisp fragrance of fresh linen. It was too warm for a quilt, or other form of covering, so she lay, naked, in the languid night air, staring into the shadows, waiting for him.

He was smiling when he came to her, easing himself on to the mattress beside her with a sigh of contentment and anticipation.

'My love. My sweet love.'

The whispered words, signalling the commencement of their private, erotic ritual.

His hand touched her breast, cupping its scented warmth, while his fingers circled the rosy nipple, making her catch her breath in instant need.

He knew exactly what he was doing. He'd always known—from that first, overwhelming time together—as if his instincts matched hers, making the desires and yearnings of their bodies identical.

She lifted her hands to his face, running her fingers pleasurably along the faint and familiar roughness of his jawline, drawing his mouth down to hers.

Lips parted, they teased each other with the tips of their tongues, brushing, caressing, retreating, enjoying the excitement of passion deliberately held in abeyance.

She slid her hands to his shoulders, and down the length of his back, relishing the strength of bone, the play of muscle under her fingertips, making him groan softly in pleasure.

Sometimes the delight of touch, the warm liquid exploration of hands and mouths contented them for half an hour or more, but this time it would not be like that, she knew.

She could feel the urgency building in him, like an underground spring, forcing its way to the surface. She moved against him, brushing her nipples with his, kissing the hollow of his throat where the pulse raged, running her fingers through the damp chest hair, then down over his flat belly to the narrow male loins.

They came together, fitted together so harmoniously, that it seemed as if their bodies had been created for no other purpose. As if, indeed, they were each the perfect half of the other.

They rose and sank together in the moist, heated rhythms and patterns of their lovemaking, each movement revealing some new discovery, some uncharted plateau of delight to be explored.

She heard herself say his name, her voice blurred and drowsy with passion, her arms tightening to draw him even nearer, hold him within her, so that he would be absorbed into her very being at the moment of fulfilment.

But her arms closed on nothing, and no one. A scream rose in her throat, and her weighted eyelids flew open as her gaze frantically raked the moonlit room, and the stark emptiness of the bed beside her.

For a moment, she lay still, letting the frantic thud of her heart against her ribcage subside a little. Then she sat up slowly, pushing back her damp cloud of hair from her face, shivering a little as she disentangled the sheet from her sweat-slicked body.

A dream, she thought, swallowing. Another dream. That was all it was. But, oh, God, it was so vivid—so real. But then, they always were.

She drew her knees up to her chin, and sat for a while. Then she left the bed, and went into the shower, adjusting the controls so that tepid water cascaded over her head and down the whole length of her body, drenching her, cleansing her. Washing the demons away.

She wrapped herself in a bath sheet, hitching it up, sarong-style, then padded into the living area. She chose a can of fruit juice from the selection in the tiny refrigerated bar, and carried it out on to the terrace. She snapped the ring pull, and emptied a long, grateful mouthful of the cold juice down her dry throat.

The can was icy, pearled with moisture from the fridge, and she rested it against her forehead for a moment, letting its coolness counteract the aching heat above her eyes.

The moon swung above her like a great benign face. The air was like a warm blanket, carrying the scent of a thousand flowers, and she breathed it deeply, leaning back on the rattan lounger, listening to the distant play of the ocean on the beach.

She knew, of course, that it was impossible to control one's dreams, but for all that she was bitterly ashamed of the sensual labyrinth her subconscious had drawn her into once more.

Particularly so when she'd just cried herself to sleep.

After Ross had left her, she'd been tormented for months with dreams like that—sensuous, arousing dreams, carrying her to the edge of consummation, then abandoning her there, solitary and sterile.

Wasn't it bad enough that, unasked and unwanted, he'd invaded her waking hours once more? Surely, dear God, she could blot him out of the darkness—prevent him creating havoc in her sleep as well.

She didn't need to be reminded of the joy they'd created together. She wanted to forget.

I've got to forget, she thought, with a little dry sob. Got to...

She was realistic enough to know that part of the problem was her self-imposed celibacy of the past four years. Although she had never been seriously tempted to break it, in spite of the attention and admiration that had been heaped on her, especially by her father's business partner, Cameron Denys.

Cameron had asked her to be his wife countless times, she thought, with an inward sigh. He was wealthy, floridly good-looking, and not without charm, but she knew she would never have accepted his proposal, even if the guilty secret of her hidden marriage hadn't stood in the way.

Maybe, one day, she might meet someone she could trust and care about enough to commit herself again. In the meantime, she supposed she could always try hypnotherapy.

She drank down the rest of her juice and sat up, wiping the faint stickiness from her lips with the back of her hand. Her mouth still felt faintly tender, she noticed, frowning.

But that, of course, was why she'd had the dream. It was all the fault of that merciless kiss Ross had inflicted on her. He'd wanted to punish her—and he'd succeeded. But why?

He was the betrayer, who'd vanished from her life with her father's pay-off. Yet he'd spoken almost as if he blamed her for his own greed and weakness. As if meeting her again had resurrected some long-buried feelings of guilt which he was trying to exorcise.

If so, surely he would be as anxious to avoid her from now on as she was to keep away from him?

Yet, 'I'll be seeing you...' His parting words had not been of separation.

It was as if he was out there, somewhere, in the velvet darkness, watching her again.

Macy shivered, and got determinedly to her feet. It was high time she went indoors, and tried to get some rest for what remained of the night. It could be a big day tomorrow. A day when she would need all her wits about her.

She felt the bath sheet slip a little, and as her hand moved to anchor it more firmly she was suddenly, crazily tempted to let it fall away completely. To walk naked down the winding path between the whispering, fragrant shrubs to the crescent of silver beach. To let the fantasy begun in her dream go on to its ultimate conclusion with the man who must surely be waiting for her—there, on the edge of the sea.

She stopped, with a sharp gasp, flinging back her head. That, she berated herself, would be a self-betrayal beyond words.

Because there was no man, no tender, sensuous lover waiting to beguile her into rapture with his words and touch, and she knew it. He'd never really existed at all—always been a figment of her imagination, and she had to remember that.

All the same, she knew she dared not go and see for herself.

She turned and fled back into the shelter of the bungalow, closing the louvred doors against the rustle of the night breeze among the leaves, and the siren call of the sea breaking on the sand.

Moon madness, Macy told herself firmly over breakfast the next day. That was all it had been. An emotional storm in a teacup which had left her drained, but composed, and able to get matters back into perspective.

But it was unpalatable but undeniable that Ross, however mercenary and worthless he might be, was still incredibly attractive with a strong sexual charisma.

The physical chemistry between them had always been a dangerously potent force, blinding her to the flaws in his character that had been clearly apparent to her father.

Although it had not been simply his faults that Sir Edwin had objected to.

Questioned directly over dinner at that first nerve-racking meeting, Ross had admitted, with a shrug, that he was illegitimate, and that his mother, now dead, had brought him up unaided as a single parent.

Macy, with a sinking heart, saw her father sitting back with an expression of almost harsh satisfaction.

'Why didn't you tell me?' she asked as they drove back to the flat.

He smiled at her. 'Because you never asked.'

'But I told you all about my family.'

'Yes.' The glance he gave her was tender. 'How your father saw this beautiful girl in a New York department store, and followed her from shop to shop until he could make an opportunity to speak to her. Which is why you were eventually christened Macy. I could never compete with that.'

'It's not a matter of competition,' she insisted, troubled.

His mouth twisted wryly. 'Isn't it? I think your father might not agree. And I'm sure he wouldn't want me to know anything as human about himself as that story.' He paused. 'Let's call it a matter of pride, and leave it at that.'

But she couldn't. 'Do you—know who your father is?'

'You mean Sir Edwin hasn't been able to find out?' The barb in his words had stung. He saw her flinch, and his voice gentled. 'No, Macy. I don't know my father at all. Now, can we drop the subject—please?'

She agreed, but the thought—the suspicion that he hadn't been completely honest with her rankled.

Looking back, Macy could see that it was a warning, a cloud on the horizon, a faint rumble of thunder on a summer day.

I should have seen then that he couldn't be trusted, she thought bleakly.

Which made it even more frightening to realise that, even after four years of heartbreak and self-regeneration, her sexual awareness of Ross was apparently as strong as ever. Shaming too, she reproached herself. How could she want, even for a moment, a man who'd used her as Ross had done?

Well, the short answer to that was—she didn't. She was going to regain control of her wayward emotions, bury the past where it belonged, and get on with the task in hand. Which was bringing off the Thunder Cay deal without further delay.

Especially as a note had been delivered along with her breakfast telling her that Mr Delancey would be sending a car for her at ten o'clock.

She drew a breath, half excited, half apprehensive. Let battle commence, she thought.

She decided to dress smart-casual, teaming a white knee-length skirt with a silky top in shades of jade and turquoise. Her hair she twisted into a thick plait. She put all the documentation she needed into a big shoulder-bag and set off for Reception.

Loud Shirt and his friends were there before her, checking out. He gave her a sullen look but said nothing, so she supposed she should be grateful to Ross for that, if nothing else.

'Miz Landin?' The clerk smiled at her. 'Your car's out front, waiting.'

She pushed open the heavy glass door and went out into the sunlight.

And stopped dead. The only car waiting was a dark blue American convertible. And leaning against it, totally at his ease in white shorts and a bronze-coloured open necked shirt, was Ross.

'So there you are,' he greeted her lazily. 'The day's half over.'

Macy's fingers tightened round the strap of her bag until her knuckles turned white, as she strove to maintain her composure.

She said icily, 'Just what is the meaning of this?'

'You were expecting a car, I think,' he said. 'Well, this is it, complete with driver. It's your lucky day.'

She shook her head. 'I don't think so. And I'm not in the mood for games.'

'Who is?' He opened the passenger door. 'Jump in, darling. Time's wasting.'

She said, 'Whatever you're up to, Ross—which I really don't want to know—it won't work. I don't require your services, now or ever. I have my own plans for today.'

'Of course.' His voice was matter of fact. 'And while I don't want to seem pressing, it's a fair drive down to Trade Winds, and Mr Hilliard isn't a man who likes to be kept waiting.'

For a moment, she looked at him blankly, as winded as if she'd been kicked in the stomach.

She said, her voice faltering a little. 'I don't know what you mean.'

His firm mouth compressed impatiently. 'Come off it, Macy. Now who's playing games? Either go with me, or stay,' he added flatly. 'The choice is yours.'

For a long moment she stared at him. There was faint amusement in the aquamarine eyes hiding something else less easy to decipher. Something disturbing.

She said slowly, 'I don't really have a choice—do I?'

'No,' he said. 'Not if you want Thunder Cay.' His smile mocked her stunned expression. 'I've told you before, Macy, this is a very small island.' He took her arm, his grasp firm, almost, she thought faintly, implacable. 'Now, let's go.'

CHAPTER FOUR

THEY drove out of the town in silence, and headed southwards.

The ocean was rarely out of sight along their route, its azure glitter glimpsed between the casuarinas which lined the dusty roadway. Apart from small, scattered fruit plantations, much of the landscape seemed to consist of scrub, interspersed with clumps of tall cacti and ferns.

The hood of the car was down, and under ordinary circumstances, Macy would have enjoyed the controlled power of the car on the well-nigh empty road, and the sensation of the cooling breeze from the sea in her face.

But she was too tautly aware of the man next to her to be able to relax. The heated sexuality of her previous night's dream was all too vivid in her mind. She found she was glancing sideways, registering the movement of his lean, strong hands on the wheel. Remembering the soaring excitement he could so easily evoke.

But she had to dismiss that from her mind, she told herself savagely. Her sole concern should be his apparent involvement with Boniface Hilliard, and familiarity with Gilmour-Denys's plans for Thunder Cay. It occurred to her that, if he wanted, Ross might be able to throw a hefty spanner in the works.

She sat staring rigidly through the windscreen, a thousand bewildered questions teeming unanswered in her head.

He said at last, 'You're very quiet.'

She offered him an icy smile. 'I have a lot to think about.'

'And I thought you were simply admiring the scenery,' Ross said mockingly. 'Talking of which, if you glance to the left, you'll see one of our main attractions—Morgan's Point.'

She turned her head unwillingly, to see a rocky headland crowned by a ruined tower, resembling a lighthouse stunted at birth.

'History says that Henry Morgan the buccaneer used it as a lookout to spot likely ships to pillage,' Ross told her. 'Want to stop and see if you can pick up any piratical vibrations?'

'I think I already have more than I can handle,' she said coolly. 'Besides, as you say, I don't want to keep Mr Hilliard waiting.

'Very understandable,' he said gravely.

They reached the turn-off some thirty minutes later. It wasn't particularly impressive. Just a single-track dirt road, barred by an elderly wooden gate, half hanging off its hinges. Presumably Boniface Hilliard was loath to spend any of his fabled wealth on such mundane matters as simple maintenance, Macy thought drily.

There was a faded sign at the side of the track, stating 'Trade Winds'. And, more dauntingly, 'Private. No admittance'.

'Can you manage the gate?' Ross requested.

Macy approached it gingerly. She touched the sagging timbers which immediately collapsed in terror back against their supporting post. She patted them kindly, amused in spite of herself.

'It's all right,' she said under her breath. 'I won't hurt you.'

She watched Ross drive through, then lifted the gate gently back into place.

'Beautifully done,' he said sardonically as she got back into the car.

'I know.' She flashed him a brilliant smile. 'And I help old ladies across the road.'

'I hope you haven't told Daddy,' he said, and she changed the smile to a glare, as the car moved forward.

The track beyond the gate was in poor condition, and led sharply upwards. Ross proceeded carefully, avoiding the worst of the ruts. When he reached the top of the slope, he braked slightly, giving her a chance to look down.

In spite of herself, Macy caught her breath in swift excitement. Beneath them was a small cove, fringed by palm trees, its sand gleaming silver in the sun. A small landing stage had been built out into the lagoon, and she could see a boat, sleek and powerful, moored beside it.

Inside the lagoon, the sea was smooth and pale turquoise, but beyond the line of creamy foam which marked the reef, it deepened to indigo and emerald.

Macy shaded her eyes, and looked out to the open sea. Half-hidden in the shimmering haze between the vivid blue of the sky and water, was a darker, almost purple smudge.

'Yes,' Ross laconically confirmed, as if she'd spoke aloud. 'That's Thunder Cay.'

Trade Winds itself lay directly below, dominating the cove. It was a big, sprawling white house without any of the grandeur she'd imagined, and set so close to the beach that the steps of the front veranda, draped in crimson bougainvillaea, descended directly on to the sand. A balcony with a wrought-iron balustrade encircled the house at first floor level, and Macy saw a woman dressed in white emerge from one of the rooms and stand, a hand shading her eyes, looking up at the car.

Ross took the car gently down the slope, and parked at the side of the house.

He glanced at Macy, brows raised. 'Ready?'

'Of course.' She hitched her bag on to her shoulder, and walked ahead of him along the veranda, and into the house.

For all his wealth, Boniface Hilliard favoured simplicity around him, she thought. The floors were of mellow golden wood, the walls painted in clear pale shades that reflected the hues of the sand, sea and sky. Furniture had been kept to a minimum, and was all very old, and undoubtedly valuable. The whole effect was one of air and space, and Macy found it immensely attractive.

Nor was it lost on her that Ross seemed completely at home there.

She ran the tip of her tongue round dry lips. If he was working for Boniface Hilliard, and in a position of trust, he'd certainly fallen on his feet. Although that wouldn't guarantee his loyalty, of course.

It certainly explained the affluence he'd displayed last night, but not the earlier beachcomber guise, she thought frowningly. Surely Mr Hilliard didn't allow his henchmen to look as if they belonged on Skid Row?

She heard a faint sound, and looked up to see a girl walking down the stairs towards them. It was the one she'd seen on the balcony, Macy realised, and much younger at close quarters than she'd originally thought. She had long blonde hair, worn in a neat top-knot, and an attractive kittenish face with wide blue eyes and a full mouth. The white dress which showed off her rounded figure to such advantage was a nurse's uniform.

She was also, Macy realised, frowningly, oddly familiar, although she could swear they'd never met . . .

'I was wondering where you were, Judy.' Ross sent her a swift smile. 'Macy, meet Nurse Ryan, our resident angel.'

The expression in the other's long-lashed eyes, as they looked Macy over, was far from angelic, and she shook hands without warmth.

'Miss Gilmour is here to see Mr Hilliard,' Ross went on. 'Can we go up now?'

Judy Ryan pursed her lips. 'I wish he wouldn't take the law into his own hands like this,' she protested. 'I'd have advised against any appointments today. It's so bad for his routine to be interrupted.'

'I think we'll have to relax the rules for once.' Ross spoke pleasantly, but an order had been given, and by the way Nurse Ryan bit her lip she knew it.

She said to Macy, 'Follow me, then, please, but keep your business brief, and try not to tire him.'

She led the way up the wide, curving staircase. She had good legs set off by smart white court shoes. Macy trailed behind her, uncomfortably aware of Ross at her shoulder. Her interview with Boniface Hilliard was not to be a private one, it seemed. But she could hardly protest until she knew what influence he had with his employer. And Ross seemed only too well acquainted with her business there anyway, she thought with a mental shrug of unhappy resignation.

THUNDER ON THE REEF 59

The room she was conducted to was clearly the master bedroom, but the master wasn't in bed. Clad in silk pyjamas and a light Paisley robe, he was lying, propped up by cushions, on a couch by the window, overlooking the sea.

Boniface Hilliard had once been a big man, but illness had diminished him, wrinkling his skin and making it hang on his bones as though he no longer fitted inside it. His hair was white and very thick, and he had the look of an outdoor man, confined against his will.

'Welcome to Trade Winds, Miss Gilmour.' His handshake was firm, but the skin felt papery. 'I was told you were a determined, single-minded young woman. Your presence here today would seem to confirm that.'

He looked past her at Ross. 'Tell Judy to bring that coffee now, boy,' he directed. 'And you, Miss Gilmour, pull up that chair.'

Macy, obeying, found she was being studied closely as she sat down. The pale blue eyes were taking in everything there was to her, but it was not a particularly friendly examination, she realised with a sense of shock. She wondered what reports Ross had made about her? Not the truth, that was for sure.

Judy Ryan appeared, carrying a tray which she set down on a table by the couch.

'Shall I pour, Mr Hilliard?' Her voice was sweetly deferential.

'No, Miss Gilmour can do it, unless such a domestic chore's beneath her.' He turned a faintly caustic eye on her as Judy Ryan left the room with something of a flounce.

'By no means.' Macy refused to be thrown.

He watched broodingly as she manipulated the heavy pot, adding cream and sugar to order, his scrutiny turning the simple task into a minor ordeal.

'You don't wear any jewellery, Miss Gilmour,' he remarked unexpectedly as she handed him his cup.

'Not during working hours, Mr Hilliard,' she returned coolly.

'But this is a social occasion.' He took a sip of the coffee, the pale eyes regarding her over the rim of the cup.

'Yes, but I hope we can combine business with pleasure.' She took a deep breath, sharply aware of Ross, who'd taken up a position by the window, arms folded across his chest. 'I understand that, in the right circumstances, Thunder Cay might be available for sale.'

He nodded, a faint smile curling his mouth. 'That's my understanding too.'

'Then I hope very much you'll allow me to put an offer from Gilmour-Denys for the property before you.'

She was doing it all wrong—playing it like a complete novice. She wouldn't be surprised if he told her to drink her coffee and go.

He was shaking his head. 'It wouldn't be proper for me to let you do that, Miss Gilmour. You see, Thunder Cay doesn't belong to me any more. It's being marketed by the new owner.'

Macy nearly dropped her cup, as shock mingled with mortification assailed her. Oh, God, she thought, shuddering, how could our information have been so inaccurate?

And what made it a hundred times worse was that Ross was there to witness her discomfiture.

She lifted her chin. 'I wasn't aware the property had been disposed of.'

'Nobody was,' Ross said. 'It was a very private transaction.' She could almost hear the smile in his voice.

I've been set up, she thought angrily. But why? She sent the two men a glittering smile. 'Then I'm sorry I've wasted your time.'

'Oh, I wouldn't say that.' Boniface Hilliard fingered his chin. 'It so happens I'm well acquainted with the new owner, and I could furnish you with an introduction.'

Macy looked at him, nonplussed. This offer of help hardly gelled with the hostility she'd felt earlier, or any of the conflicting vibrations in the room. Yet she couldn't afford to turn it down.

She said, slowly, 'That's very kind, but...'

'But you're wondering why I went to the trouble of having you brought here first?' He shook his head again. 'When you get to my age, Miss Gilmour, a visit from a beautiful young woman is a rare and refreshing treat. And you have more than your share of looks, as I'm sure you know.'

Macy's face was burning. She was sincerely glad that Judy Ryan hadn't been around to hear that little speech. It wasn't what she'd expected him to say, nor was she sure, judging by Ross's cynical grin, that he even meant it. 'Mr Hilliard,' she began uncomfortably.

'But I won't embarrass you any more,' he went on. 'You'll want to get over to Thunder Cay.'

'You mean—go there—today?' Macy's head was whirling.

'That's where the current owner lives,' he returned.

'I didn't know it was inhabited.'

'I used to live there myself, in a house I built on the beach,' he said. 'It's basic, but it's a good place to escape to when you're under pressure.'

Macy gave him a level look. 'I can't imagine you ever running away, Mr Hilliard.'

He chuckled. 'Oh, you'd be surprised, Miss Gilmour. You'd be surprised.' He turned his head. 'Ross, you can take Miss Gilmour over to the island in *Sweet Bird*.'

'Of course,' Ross said laconically. 'As soon as she's ready.'

Oh, no, Macy thought, with a sense of dread. She said hurriedly, 'A simple letter of introduction would do. I can make my own arrangements.'

'We wouldn't hear of it. Strike while the iron's hot. There's never a better time than the present to make a deal.'

She couldn't argue with that, at least.

'We want your visit to Fortuna to be a complete success,' Boniface Hilliard continued. 'Isn't that so, Ross? We don't attract the tourists like Paradise Island, maybe, but those of us who live here feel it has its own charm.'

'Perhaps Miss Gilmour hasn't had sufficient time to appreciate it,' Ross put in silkily.

'I've had plenty, thanks.' She didn't look at him. 'Far more than I anticipated. Anyway Fortuna's tourist industry could stand to benefit from Gilmour-Denys's plans for Thunder Cay. The kind of leisure facility we envisage is bound to have spin-offs for the adjoining islands.'

'Like a big, fat spider in a web,' Ross said softly. 'What makes you think that Thunder Cay should be exploited in this way, Macy?'

She said, 'That's something I prefer to discuss with the present owner.'

'I hope there won't be too many changes.' Boniface Hilliard leaned back against his pillows. 'My family has been connected with this island since the seventeenth century, when Old Bevis made himself governor here—or that's what he called himself. He had no lawful authority from the king or anyone else. I guess really he was just a goddamn pirate—a freebooter. Some people say that's what I am too—just a twentieth-century

version of Old Bevis.' He gave a hoarse chuckle.
'Although I've built up my fortune from the
world stock markets rather than Spanish gold.'

Macy was interested despite herself. 'I saw the
statue of him in town,' she said. 'Near your
lawyer's office. I realised he must be a relation
of yours.'

'Careful, Macy,' Ross cut in silkily. 'You're
interested in real estate, remember, not human
beings.'

She said curtly, 'I didn't know the two were
incompatible,' and replaced her cup on the tray.

Judy Ryan's arrival was almost a relief. 'It's
time for your medication, Mr Hilliard.'

'And a hint that we should leave you in peace,'
Ross said. He put a hand on the older man's
shoulder, and pressed it quietly, then looked at
Macy. 'Are you ready?'

She hesitated. She didn't feel ready at all, especially to go with him. The new turn of events
had thrown her off balance. Besides, there were
strange undercurrents—tensions in the room that
she didn't understand.

But if she had to go to Thunder Cay to make
the deal, she would. She could stand a few more
hours.

She said, 'If I could just use the bathroom?'

'Of course.' Boniface Hilliard waved a hand.
'Show her, Judy.'

Macy said an awkward 'Goodbye,' and followed the other girl reluctantly down the passage.

The room she was shown was at the other end of the house, and obviously part of a little used guest suite. A deliberate choice, no doubt, she thought with irony.

Judy Ryan looked round with raised brows.

'I think everything's here—soap—towels.' From her tone, Macy suspected she would have liked to have added 'Polyfilla.'

She said neutrally, 'Thank you.'

'I presume you can find your own way downstairs? Good. Then I can return to my patient.' Nurse Ryan whisked herself away, leaving Macy wondering once again where and how she could possibly have seen her before.

That, however, was the least of her problems, she thought, turning on the cold tap in the basin and letting the water stream over the uneasy pulses in her wrists.

She supposed she'd just passed some unofficial vetting procedure, although Mr Hilliard clearly had no right to do any such thing. Presumably, he felt a strong involvement still with Thunder Cay, in spite of it belonging to someone else.

How on earth could we have missed such a thing? she wondered helplessly.

The last fifteen minutes had been no picnic by anyone's standards. In fact, she looked distinctly wan, she decided grimly, adding a touch of blusher to her cheekbones, and renewing the subdued coral on her mouth. If she was going to be forced to spend even more time in Ross's company, then she would do so with all flags flying.

She made her way back to the stairs, and was just about to begin her descent, when she glanced down into the hall below.

Ross was there, and Judy Ryan was with him, standing close enough to touch, her hand on his arm as she talked to him in a low voice, her face intense.

'So much for patient care,' Macy remarked under her breath, then paused. There was something hauntingly familiar about the little tableau. Something buried deep in her memory, now pushing its way again to the surface.

Photographs, she thought, spilling across a table, and her hand, pushing them away in revulsion, not wanting to look.

'See for yourself what he's like.' Her father's voice, ringing in her head, in grim triumph.

And her anguished gaze taking in at last the couple at the table. The girl's blonde head so close to Ross's dark one. The way her body leaned towards him, the tips of her full breasts brushing the sleeve of his jacket. The almost drugged sensuality in the kittenish face.

Then, she thought, watching the pair below her with curious detachment, as now.

And heard her own voice, choking on the words. 'Take them away. Isn't it bad enough that he's gone—that he's left me—without these? Couldn't you leave me with anything?'

Shock rooted her to the spot. She felt numb, and sick to her stomach at the same time.

Ross and Judy Ryan together in London all those years ago, she thought faintly. Ross and Judy Ryan here together now. It couldn't be possible. Her memory must be playing tricks.

It was all too much of a coincidence, unless, of course, it was no coincidence at all. Unless Ross had left Britain with the other girl, as well as his pay-off, and stayed with her all this time.

Carefully, Macy edged away from the pain beginning to build inside her.

Why should she care anyway? she flayed herself with angry bitterness. Her marriage was over long ago. Ross's relationship with the blonde nurse, or any other woman, was no concern of hers.

But as Judy Ryan's arms went up to draw Ross possessively down to her kiss, Macy snapped out of her trance and stepped backwards, so that the pair of them were hidden from her by the curve of the staircase.

Because, she realised with a commingling of fear and bewildered anguish, the sight of Ross in another woman's arms was still an agony she could not bear to endure.

And the implications of that she dared not even contemplate.

CHAPTER FIVE

As *Sweet Bird* cut effortlessly through the sparkling water, Macy stared rigidly ahead of her at the rocky bulk of Thunder Cay, getting closer with every minute that passed.

She was still in turmoil from that devastating moment of self-revelation in the hall at Trade Winds. Her impulse had been to cut and run. To let the deal on Thunder Cay go by default.

But she hadn't the physical means to leave, she realised tautly, as she waited at the head of the stairs, her nails scoring the palms of her hands, her mind trying to blot out the image of the two, below her, locked passionately in each other's arms. She was dependent on Ross for transport, so she was, to some extent, trapped.

Besides, the last thing she wanted was for Ross to know that anything he said or did had the power to affect her in any way. Pride, if not self-preservation, demanded that at least.

What she couldn't understand was why he hadn't ended their brief and secret marriage himself. If he'd been involved with another woman all this time, why hadn't he asked for a discreet divorce, instead of allowing things to drag on like this? Perhaps he was secretly ashamed of the way he'd treated her. If so, he was hiding it very well, she thought, anger slashing across the desolation inside her.

When she had eventually ventured downstairs, the hall was empty. From the open door, she could see Ross on the landing stage, loading some cartons and a couple of canvas bags on board the boat, helped by a tall black man in khaki shorts and shirt.

She didn't want Ross as a travelling companion again, but what choice did she have? And at least this time she wouldn't be alone with him, she tried to reassure herself.

She couldn't avoid flinching as he took her hand to help her on board, and saw his mouth set grimly as he absorbed her reaction.

But all he said was, 'Meet Sam, Mr Hilliard's right-hand man.'

'I thought that was you,' she returned coolly, returning Sam's smile as his big hand engulfed hers warmly.

'Far from it. I'm a comparative newcomer to the set-up.'

The fringe benefits were fantastic, she thought, as Sam started the engine. Use of a very expensive car, and now this boat, big, streamlined and reeking of money. Ross had certainly fallen on his feet.

'Here.' Ross handed her a dilapidated straw hat with a broad brim. 'You'll need this.'

'The sun doesn't bother me,' she dismissed, adding shortly. 'Please don't fuss.'

'As you wish. I just hope you don't regret it.' Ross tossed the hat down on to the cushioned seat.

I hope so too, she thought. I already have more regrets than I can handle.

It was largely a silent trip. Apart from asking her if she was comfortable, Ross seemed lost in his own thoughts. And Sam was content to hum gently under his breath at the wheel as he drove the powerful boat through the water.

For her part, Macy kept her attention fixed firmly on the approaching island, concentrating so hard that, in the end, her head began to ache.

Unobtrusively, she lifted her hands, and rubbed her temples gently with her fingertips.

'You should be wearing that hat,' Ross said flatly. So he'd noticed what she was doing.

'I'm fine,' she fibbed, not looking at him, but tinglingly aware of his proximity—altogether too close for comfort.

'Nice to know you're impervious to the elements as well as everything else,' Ross returned. His tone was silky, but there was an edge to it. 'But the fact remains, you aren't used to this kind of heat.' He nodded towards the island. 'Well, there you are—journey's end.'

But no lovers meeting. The words spun crazily in and out of her mind. Macy Gilmour, she berated herself, you're pathetic.

'Yes, at last,' she returned shortly. 'I'll be glad to get the deal sewn up.'

'You think your terms will be accepted?'

'I certainly hope so. It's a fair offer.'

'No doubt your father shares your ambition. I hear Gilmour-Denys have been struggling of late.'

'You shouldn't listen to silly gossip.' She stiffened. 'The company's in good shape.'

'Really?' he said politely. 'Then it hasn't over-extended its borrowing on the strength of acquiring Thunder Cay for the consortium?'

'Absolutely not.' Or has it? she wondered, remembering her father's edginess and unwonted anxiety. But even if Gilmour-Denys had problems, she was certainly not prepared to discuss them with Ross of all people.

She hurried into speech. 'Are you going to tell me something about the new owner?'

'What do you want to know?'

'Well, for one thing, how he got in ahead of the field, and persuaded Mr Hilliard to sell to him.' She paused. 'And how the sale was kept so quiet.'

'There was no actual sale,' he said. 'Thunder Cay was made over to him by deed of gift.'

She turned sharply, aware of a jab of pain across her forehead. 'What? But you don't give away a valuable piece of property like that.'

'You do,' he said, 'if it's to your only son.'

Shock silenced her. Then she drew a breath. 'But that's nonsense,' she protested. 'Boniface Hilliard has no children. Everyone knows that.'

'Then everyone is wrong,' he said calmly. 'He has a son and heir, and presently you'll meet him.'

'But you can't keep something like that quiet. Why hasn't the Press got hold of it?'

His smile was tight-lipped. 'Boniface has never welcomed intrusion into his affairs—public or private. Don't let the laid-back attitude at Trade Winds fool you, darling. The place is a fortress. If you'd arrived uninvited, you wouldn't have got past the rickety gate.'

The engine note changed, as Sam throttled back.

'And now we have our own rickety gate to negotiate,' Ross added casually, pointing to the restless line of surf breaking just ahead of them. 'Quite a narrow gap in the reef. Something to bear in mind if Gilmour-Denys are planning a marina.'

It was certainly a delicate operation, getting *Sweet Bird* into the lagoon, and Macy winced as she heard the keel scraping across coral.

'Don't worry 'bout a thing.' Sam slanted a grin at her. 'We've got enough wrecks in these parts. I don't aim to add this beauty to them, no ma'am.'

'I'm glad to hear it.' She realised shamefacedly that she'd been holding her breath.

But any development carried out at Thunder Cay would demand a better access than that, she thought. It might even be necessary to blast a bigger gap in the coral, although she dared not consider what damage that would do the myriad life-forms supported by the reef.

But that wasn't up to her, she reminded herself. That would be Cameron's ultimate decision, and if he'd ever been interested in green issues and the environment it was news to her.

She just had to conduct the preliminaries with the stranger who was waiting for them. Although why he should want to dispose of his father's gift was a mystery beyond her comprehension.

Safely inside the lagoon, she peered eagerly forward. The island was much greener than she'd anticipated, and not nearly as flat as Fortuna. The hinterland seemed almost rugged, by contrast. She could make out the house too, a solid wooden single-storey construction with a thatched roof, sheltered by the palm trees that fringed the wide crescent of silver sand. But no sign of life. She'd imagined the lone resident would have come down to meet them.

'Romantic, isn't it?' Ross came to stand beside her as Sam turned the boat towards the primitive landing stage. 'The perfect place for a honeymoon.'

'If you say so,' she returned shortly.

'Oh, I do,' he said softly. 'Imagine it, Macy— total seclusion to enjoy each other. No need to dress for dinner—or anything else. Nothing on your skin but the warmth of the sun, and the glory of the moon.'

His voice lingered over the words, creating tantalising sensuous images, and to her annoyance she felt a sudden betraying heat in her face.

Her voice was taut. 'We should let you write the brochure.'

He laughed. 'Always the businesswoman.'

Not always, she thought. Once I was trusting—vulnerable. Until you taught me differently...

Sam brought *Sweet Bird* gently to rest beside the small jetty. Ross jumped ashore to tie up, and Macy scrambled after him.

Without the noise of the engine, the island seemed not merely secluded, but suddenly, hauntingly quiet, she thought with a faint shiver.

She looked uncertainly at Ross, and found him watching her, his eyes intent, a faint smile playing about his mouth. He said quietly, 'Welcome to Thunder Cay.'

She glanced away hurriedly, aware her pulses had quickened, shading her eyes with her hand, her brows drawing together. 'There doesn't seem to be anyone around.'

'There will be. Go on up to the house,' Ross directed, as he and Sam began to unload the various cartons.

She hitched her bag on to her shoulder, and started up the beach, her feet sinking into the yielding sand. She felt as if a heavy weight had been placed on her skull and was pressing her downwards. A cold drink, she thought longingly, and a seat in the shade. Then she'd be fighting fit again.

She was halfway up the beach when she heard *Sweet Bird*'s engine roar into life again. She swung round, and saw the boat reversing, then heading back towards the reef and the open sea beyond, while Ross stood on the jetty, waving goodbye.

For a moment Macy stood, open-mouthed in sheer disbelief, then she began to run back the way she'd come, yelling and waving her arms, screaming at Sam to come back.

Ross watched her, hands on hips, his face unsmiling.

He said, 'It's no use, Macy. He obeys my orders, not yours. And he'll return when I tell him, and not before.'

'And when will that be?' she demanded tautly.

'All in good time.' The aquamarine eyes studied her dispassionately. 'Relax, Macy. Enjoy the ambience. You're planning a resort where people can get away from it all. Test it for yourself.'

There was a sharp, tingling silence, and she was the first to look away.

She said, 'If this is a joke, it's in very poor taste.'

'It's all perfectly serious,' he returned. He slung the canvas bags over his shoulder, and walked towards her. 'You and I have a deal to negotiate.' He paused. 'As well as the unfinished business I mentioned last night.'

'We have a deal?' In spite of the intense heat, she felt suddenly deathly cold. 'I don't understand.'

'Don't you? I thought you'd have put two and two together by now, and come up with an answer,' he said. 'But come up to the house and I'll explain in full.' He gave her a critical glance. 'In spite of your protests, you look as if you've had quite enough sun for one day.'

She said between her teeth, 'I'm not moving a step. You can explain right here, and it had better be good. You have no right to kidnap me and dump me here on someone else's property.'

'For the record,' he said slowly, 'I'm your husband, which gives me any rights I choose to assume.'

Her heart seemed to stop momentarily. She said thickly, 'It's a little late to remember that.'

'On the contrary, darling.' His voice slowed to a drawl. 'I've never forgotten it, even for a moment, during this long separation.' He paused, the cool blue gaze holding her—mesmerising her. 'And, also for the record,' he went on quietly, 'this is not someone else's property. Thunder Cay belongs to me.'

'That's nonsense.' Her voice wavered. 'You're lying—you have to be. You said on the boat that it belonged to Boniface Hilliard's son...'

'All perfectly true.' He made her a mock bow, smiling at her sharp intake of breath. 'Ross Bannister Hilliard, at your service.'

'What?' Her voice rose. 'You're actually claiming to be his son? Since when?'

'Since the moment of conception, I presume.' He shrugged. 'Isn't that the biological norm?'

'Please don't equate yourself with any kind of normal behaviour,' she hit back at him. 'What is this? Some kind of confidence trick to get yourself yet another stack of unearned income?'

'No,' he said. 'I have all the documentation to prove what I say, and to confirm my ownership of this island. Now, come on up to the house and we'll talk.'

'Never,' she said. 'All deals are off. I'm going back to Fortuna right now.'

'It's a long swim,' he said. 'Watch out for barracuda. Or maybe they should watch out for you.'

'I am not joking.' Her voice was angry.

'Nor am I, Macy. Without a boat you're going nowhere.' He walked past her up the beach. 'Now, I'm going in the house for a cold beer. You, of course, can stay there and melt, if that's what you want.'

'I'm not moving until the boat comes back for me,' she said defiantly.

His brows lifted, and he began to laugh. 'In that case you certainly will melt. I told Sam to come back for us in a week.'

'Oh, God.' Her voice cracked. 'It can't be true...'

'Stay there and wait,' Ross advised crisply. 'You'll find out. I'll throw food to you at appropriate times, of course. If you plan to face seawards, the first thing to hit you in the back of the head will be dinner.'

He turned and went up the rickety steps to the veranda. After a long moment of indecision, she followed. She was scared, but standing on the beach in splendid isolation would solve nothing. Besides, the heat was making her feel swimmy and faintly sick.

She found herself confronted by a combined kitchen and living area. There was a shabby sofa, and an enormous table, its surface littered with papers.

Ross dropped the bags on the table then sauntered to the large refrigerator and extracted two bottles of beer. He offered her one, which she declined, in spite of her thirst, with a curt shake of the head.

She looked round slowly, assimilating her surroundings. There were only two rooms apparently leading off the living area. One of them, as she could see through its curtained archway, was a bedroom. The other preserved its privacy behind a solid-looking door. A lean-to extension at the rear housed the toilet and shower.

And that seemed to be it. The simple life, she thought, that all at once seemed incredibly complicated—even threatening.

Ross uncapped one of the bottles and swallowed some beer, his aquamarine gaze coolly reflective as he studied her.

He said, 'You look stunned, darling. Take a seat before you fall down.'

'Is it any wonder?' She sat down at the table, glaring at him. 'I don't know what your game is, Ross, but I'm not taken in by it. I don't think you're related to Mr Hilliard in any way. You've just tricked your way into his affections somehow.' Just as you tricked me, she thought with anguish. 'He's old and ill,' she went on. 'An easy touch for a plausible story.'

'On the contrary, my sweet.' He drank some more beer, his eyes never leaving her face. 'Boniface may be physically frail, but mentally he could still buy and sell the world. I'm his son all right. And whether you accept it or not doesn't alter a thing.'

'You lied anyway,' she accused. 'You told me you didn't know who your father was.'

'No, Macy.' Ross shook his head. 'I said I didn't know him at all—a different thing from merely being aware of his identity.'

'Which you were?' she demanded, and, as he nodded silently. 'How long have you known it?'

'Since my mother's last illness,' he said quietly. 'The drugs they gave her made her ramble—say things she wasn't aware of—that she'd kept hidden all her life. When she died, I found letters that she'd kept. Photographs. A whole past locked away.'

'How convenient.'

'Not really. For a long time I didn't know what to do about it.'

'But you came up with the right answer in the end,' Macy said, with a bite. 'Tell me something. If you knew you were the only son of a multi-millionaire, why did you take the money to walk out of my life?'

'Call it a redundancy payment,' he said, his mouth curling. 'A fee for services rendered—anything you want.'

'Your golden handshake must have come as a pleasant surprise to him,' she said. 'A freelance photographer, living from hand to mouth, might not have been nearly so welcome.'

She paused. That earlier feeling of nausea had increased and intensified, and her head was throbbing, but she persevered. 'So when did you go for the jackpot—break the happy news to Daddy?'

'I didn't.' His tone was crisp. 'He found me. He'd promised my mother he would never come to look for her until he was free to marry her. Ironically, she and his wife died within weeks of each other, and I'd moved on, anyway, so the trail went cold.'

'Yet here you are—living happily ever after,' Macy said. 'What happened?'

'He became ill,' Ross said. 'Also frightened. And lonely.'

'You're breaking my heart.' A wave of giddiness swept over her, and she leaned back, searching vainly for a breath of cool air from the open door.

'That I doubt.' There was sudden harshness in his voice.

'But your new-found wealth and status don't alter a thing,' she went on. 'I insist on going back to Fortuna.'

'And so you will,' he said softly. 'Eventually. When we've agreed our deal. I was short on bargaining power in the old days. Now I'm not. I have something you want, and you're going to pay for it.' He paused. 'In one way or another.'

'What are you talking about?' She could feel panic settling like a stone in her chest.

'Why, this desirable piece of real estate you've come so far to see—what else?' He was mocking her, and she knew it. There was more—far more going on here than a simple land deal.

'I refuse to discuss it here,' she said curtly. 'I prefer more civilised surroundings.'

He shook his head. 'Can't oblige. This is as civilised as it gets.'

She stared at him. 'You can't seriously intend to keep me here.'

'Ah, but I can,' he said softly. 'And I shall.'

'You bastard,' she said hoarsely.

His smile tautened. 'Ain't that the truth? If this is your idea of conducting negotiations, Macy, thank God you never joined the diplomatic service.'

'But what do you hope to gain?' she demanded hoarsely. 'Are you holding me to ransom—trying to force my father to pay more?'

'It always comes down to money with you, Macy.' The note of contempt in his voice stung her. 'No. This time it doesn't concern your father at all, but mine. Through circumstances beyond his control, he never held me as a baby, or played with me as a child, or talked to me as a boy growing up. We both missed out on a hell of a lot. Now, it seems there may be a limit on the amount of time he has left. And before he dies he wants to hold his grandchild—someone of his own flesh and blood—in his arms.'

The aquamarine eyes held hers inexorably. Impossible to resist—or even look away, Macy thought dazedly. Her own gaze was beginning to blur, putting him somehow out of focus. His voice too seemed to be coming from some far distance.

'That's why we're here, Macy. To take the honeymoon we never had. To give our marriage a second chance, and, perhaps, give my father the grandchild he longs for.'

She pushed her chair back, and got to her feet. She needed to speak, to tell him he was crazy, but the words wouldn't form on her dry lips. She wanted to turn and run, but it was as if she was anchored there.

The room was swinging round her, spinning faster and faster until it was out of control, drawing her down into some spiralling vortex where only darkness waited.

Her invisible bonds relaxed. She heard herself say, 'No,' her voice high and terrified like a child's. Then felt herself slip down, without haste, into the welcoming blackness.

CHAPTER SIX

THERE was fire in the darkness, a stifling heat which consumed her. She was lying on the burning sand, lifting her face to the pitiless sky in a futile search for rainclouds, knowing that the coolness of the sea was only yards away, yet unable to drag herself to it.

Faces swam on the borders of her consciousness. Her father's face, and Cameron's, their expressions intent as they assembled toy building blocks into a model of a hotel complex which spread and spread until it filled the room, pushing her aching body back against the wall.

Can't you see me? she screamed at them, as they began to blur and fade. Don't you know I'm here? Help me, please.

But all that emerged was a hoarse croak.

There was a girl's face too, pretty and petulant under curling blonde hair, with a look in her eyes which made Macy shrink inside her aching skin.

And there was the man, with eyes as pale as aquamarine, and a line of dark stubble along his tanned jaw. His was the face she saw most of all.

And he was her enemy. It was because of him that she was hurting so badly. In some dim corner of her mind she knew this, and tried to struggle—

to hide somewhere in the hot sand each time he swam into focus. She had to fight him—to escape at all costs.

From some long and aching distance, she heard her voice, small and exhausted, say, 'Don't leave me.'

He said brusquely, 'I'm going nowhere. Drink this.'

His shoulder was hard under her cheek, the cotton shirt he wore rasping against the fevered tenderness of her skin. But the fruit juice he made her swallow was like nectar in her parched throat.

Her eyelids felt drugged with heaviness, but she forced them open somehow, and stared round her. The first thing she realised was that she was alone. The second, that the room was totally unfamiliar with plain board walls, and uncurtained windows, shuttered against the sun. Apart from the bed, it contained a chest of drawers with a mirror above it and a chair.

And the third, and most startling realisation was that she was in the bed, and she was naked.

Macy sat up, galvanised into shocked reaction, despite the instant reproach of her still aching body. Remembrance began to return, slowly and equally painfully.

It was not all a bad dream, as she'd hoped. And she was not safe in her bungalow at the Fortuna Bay hotel at all.

Far from it, in fact.

Ross, she thought, horrified, a faint film of sweat breaking out on her forehead. Oh, God— Ross.

As if she'd spoken his name aloud, he appeared in the doorway, leaning a negligent shoulder against the frame as he surveyed her. He was wearing faded red shorts and nothing else, and he looked devastating, she thought, her stomach lurching in swift, betraying acknowledgement.

'Welcome back to the real world,' he said silkily, the cool eyes travelling down her body.

Macey gasped, hurriedly dragging the sheet up to cover her bare breasts, a gesture which brought a faintly derisive smile to his mouth.

'It's a little late for that. And your body is hardly a mystery to me anyway.'

'What am I doing here?' she demanded huskily. 'What's happened to me?'

'Don't be silly, Macy,' he said. 'You remember perfectly well. You've had sunstroke, not amnesia.'

She swallowed. 'Is that what it was—just the sun?'

'Don't underestimate it,' he said. 'Your temperature was sky-high, and you were delirious. I had to sponge you down with cool water every few hours.'

To her annoyance, Macy found herself blushing. 'Was that strictly necessary?' She invested her voice with extra ice to compensate for her embarrassment.

'Entirely,' he said. 'I radioed Trade Winds for advice, and Judy told me what to do.'

'Of course,' she said tonelessly, cringing inwardly at the thought of the pair of them discussing her helplessness.

But a radio, she thought. Ross had a radio. On which she could transmit a message perhaps. Reach the authorities on Fortuna and make them send a boat to her rescue. Get her out of here at all costs.

'Don't raise your hopes, Macy,' Ross said, just as if she'd spoken the thought aloud. 'You'll never find it.'

'You can't keep me here against my will.' She glared at him, hating him for reading her so easily. 'I'll get out of here somehow.'

'Then you'd better start swimming,' he said pleasantly. 'The sharks will be delighted.'

She repressed a shudder, her hands tightening on the sheet. It was no good getting angry, she thought. Better by far to reason with him.

'Ross—you can't have meant all those foolish things you said—when was it?—yesterday?'

'Three days ago, actually,' he said, smiling ironically at her gasp of shock. 'And I meant every word.'

'But it's impossible—insane . . .' She heard her voice begin to shake, and controlled it with an effort. 'You're not thinking straight, Ross. I—I can understand why you want to provide your father with a grandchild—but not this way. You and I were finished long ago. We can divorce quietly as soon as you want—we don't need to worry about the grounds as it's past two years since we separated—and you can find someone else—marry her.' She tried to smile, crushing down the painful image of Judy Ryan. 'There won't be any shortage of potential brides.'

'Why? Because I'm a wealthy man now, instead of a struggling photographer?' His voice bit.

'No,' she said, in a low voice. 'I didn't mean that.'

'Not that it matters,' Ross went on almost casually. 'As I already have a wife.' The aquamarine eyes held hers making it impossible for her to look away. 'And no time to spare for a lengthy courtship, anyway. Boniface's health, as I've told you, isn't good.'

'Does he know?' she demanded rigidly. 'Have you told him who I am, and what you intend.'

'Naturally.'

'And he approves?'

Ross shrugged. 'Not entirely.'

'I'm relieved to hear it,' Macy said between her teeth.

'You decided his only son wasn't good enough for you, Macy. You can hardly expect him to accept you with open arms.'

She gasped. 'That's not what I mean, and you know it.'

'But he's a pragmatist,' Ross continued as if she hadn't spoken. 'He recognises I have little choice. And anyway, you owe me.'

'In what possible way?' she demanded huskily.

'Four years ago we were married,' he said, almost dispassionately. 'It follows that, by now, we might already have had a child. Could even have been expecting another. You were keen on a family, if my memory serves. We both were. I can remember you clinging to me, while we were making love, telling me that you wanted my baby.'

'Stop it.' Macy put her hands to her ears. 'That was a long time ago. We're not the same people any more.'

'Having slept next to you for the past couple of nights,' he said, 'old times don't seem so far away. Except that you're even lovelier, if that's possible.'

Macy's heart missed a beat. 'I was ill,' she said slowly. 'You knew that, yet you actually slept—here—in this bed?'

'There wasn't much choice,' he said. 'As well as bathing, you needed constant drinks and attention.' He paused. 'And this is the only bed.'

'Is it now.' Macy fought the wave of heat threatening to engulf her. 'Well, from now on I shall sleep on the beach.'

'I don't recommend it,' he said. 'The no-seeums will eat you alive.'

'The what?' Her voice lifted to a squeak.

'They're a kind of sand-flea,' he explained. 'Bite like hell.'

'I don't care.' Her throat was tight. 'You can't make me stay here. You can't force me to do this. Rape is still a criminal offence, even if your fore-bears were pirates.'

He said gently, 'There's no question of rape, Macy, as we both know perfectly well. And as I shall take endless pleasure in reminding you.'

A shiver convulsed her. 'Don't,' she said huskily.

The cool eyes swept her mockingly. 'What's the matter, Macy,' he taunted. 'Am I rather too close to the truth?'

'No,' she said. 'You just disgust me, that's all.'

'That's not my intention,' he said. 'I want a reawakening—a rekindling of all we used to feel for each other.'

'That's impossible.'

He shook his head. 'I don't think so. When I kissed you that night on Fortuna, you trembled in my arms.'

'That was rage,' Macy spat at him.

He laughed. 'Truly?' he drawled. 'Then you have my permission to be as angry as you like whenever you wish.'

There was a silence. Then she said thickly, 'Ross—don't do this. Please.'

'Not a word I expected to hear from you, darling.' His voice was dry. 'That heatstroke must really have taken it out of you. Don't forget, you came here to do a deal. It's not quite the one you expected, that's all. But Thunder Cay can still be yours. A belated wedding gift, if you like.'

'But only if I—do what you want.' She forced the words from the tightness in her throat.

'Of course.' His tone was matter of fact.

'How can you live with yourself?' She lifted her chin, tried to stare him down.

Ross shrugged again. 'Isn't it a pre-divorce duty of couples to seek a reconciliation?' he challenged. 'That's what I'm asking, Macy. You won't be forced or rushed into anything, I give you my word. I can wait.'

'Very reassuring,' she said bitterly, and his mouth tightened.

'Nevertheless, that's the way it's going to be, my sweet. Gentle persuasion.' His voice was quiet, almost reminiscent. 'Just the two of us alone here together. No intrusive elements, or outside interference. I've told Sam that our stay here is going to be extended indefinitely, so you'll have plenty of time to think.' He pushed himself away from the door post.

'What about my own powers of persuasion,' Macy flung at him, as he turned away. 'Suppose I convince you that our marriage is a lost cause? That you should let me go?'

Ross slanted a brief smile at her. 'You can always try,' he said softly, and left her, slumped against the pillows, staring after him.

She felt as if she'd just taken part in the London marathon. But then, looking back, life with Ross had always been like that—lived at speed, sweeping her along, imbuing her with a feeling of recklessness—a sense of risk. Leaving her often breathless.

But she couldn't think like that, she reminded herself, her heart like a stone in her chest. There was not and never could be again any life with Ross.

This—abduction was sheer bluff. He didn't—couldn't intend to keep her here. Couldn't possibly think they could resurrect their dead marriage after what he had done.

It had to be a ploy, she told herself, a scheme to extract more money from Gilmour-Denys for Thunder Cay. Ross's way of revenging himself on the man responsible for his exposure.

Macy swallowed. Her father would be expecting to hear from her. What on earth would he say—and do, when he discovered where she was, and in what company? The truth about her marriage was bound to come out, and he would be hurt. And if the Press got wind of all this, there would be the kind of scandal and notoriety Gilmour-Denys had always avoided.

She hardly dared imagine what Cameron's reaction would be, she thought with foreboding. He was always so correct in his behaviour, so narrow in his expectations of others. That was why, in spite of his determined courtship, she had always known she could never marry him, even though she was going against her father's dearest wish by refusing.

Ross reappeared in the doorway. 'I'm getting lunch,' he said. 'Can you make it to the table, or would you prefer a tray?'

'I'd prefer to get up,' she said instantly. She was too vulnerable like this. She distrusted the enforced intimacy of the situation.

'Good,' he said. 'Later, if you feel up to it, I'll show you a little of this valuable piece of property—this hidden corner of the Garden of Eden.'

The words sank into a taut silence as Macy digested them—recognised them as part of the draft brochure Cameron had already prepared for the Thunder Cay development. There wasn't much he didn't know, she thought, seething. He'd been ahead of her every step of the way.

'You must want to see the island,' he went on. 'After all, that's why you agreed to come here.'

'And what a mistake that was.' She gave him a flat look. 'This may be Eden, but I have no plans to play Eve. I'd like my clothes back.'

'Certainly.' Ross grinned at her. 'Although the alternative has its appeal.'

He disappeared momentarily, and returned with an armful of garments which he dumped on the end of the bed. 'They've been washed and dried, but not ironed,' he added. 'I don't go in for those refinements.'

'You astonish me,' she said acidly.

After all the intimacies of the past few days, it was odd that she should find the idea of him doing her personal laundry a disturbing one.

We used to share trips to the launderette in the old days, she reminded herself. Why should this be different?

She said, 'I would also appreciate some privacy. Or do you intend to watch me.'

'That also has its appealing side,' he said. 'But, as I said, I can wait.'

He unlooped the door curtain and let it fall into place.

Macy realised she'd been holding her breath, and released it slowly, in a little nervous sigh.

She was being allowed to dress in peace, but that curtain only gave an illusion of privacy, and she knew it. She was in Ross's hands—under his control.

When he said 'I can wait', it wasn't just a warning. More a declaration of intent.

She'd never actually seen this ruthless side of him when they lived together, but of course it had always been there. It had surfaced when he'd left her like that. No goodbye. Just a cold-blooded receipt for the money signed 'with thanks'.

God, how that had hurt.

Yet it seemed he'd resented being recognised for what he was and bought off. Now, he was in a position to enjoy his revenge. Because that was all this was—all it could be, Macy told herself feverishly. He'd walked out. She owed him nothing. The days and nights when she'd given herself to him with joy and abandon were long past. Now her body was her own again, and it would stay that way. She'd learned too well the agony that passion could inflict in its wake.

Nor was she prepared to allow herself to be used as some kind of brood mare, she thought, with icy determination.

Ross could only keep her on Thunder Cay for a limited time. If she wasn't in contact with Gilmour-Denys very soon, her father, not to mention Cameron, would come looking for her. And a kidnapping scandal would damage the Hilliard name as well, or more.

'The food's ready.' Ross's voice reached from the other side of the curtain. 'Are you?'

'Nearly.' Macy scrambled out of bed, and stood for a moment fighting a slight lightheadedness. After the fevered nightmares she'd been suffering, she was astounded she could feel so well.

I must have amazing powers of recuperation, she thought drily. And I'm going to need every last one of them.

Thanks to manmade fibres, her clothes were only a little creased, but Macy suspected she would be sick of the sight of them before her enforced stay came to an end.

There was a brush and comb on the chest of drawers. As well as undressing her, Ross must have unplaited her hair, she realised, as she dealt, wincing, with the tangled strands. He'd always liked her to wear it loose, stroking its burnished silkiness as it tumbled across the pillow...

She gave a vicious tug to a particularly recalcitrant knot, calling her thoughts to order. She had to be strong and single-minded if she was going to get out of this highly charged situation unscathed.

One moment of weakness, and she could be lost forever.

Not that she looked capable of punching her way out of a paper bag, she thought, grimacing. Her reflection showed her looking totally drained, her eyes enormous and her cheekbones far too prominent.

But maybe that wasn't such a bad thing, she thought with sudden excitement. Perhaps she could use the fragility of her appearance to her own advantage.

She put a hand to her head, as if warding off a dizzy spell, and studied the effect under her lashes. Not bad, she decided critically, but she must be careful not to overdo it, or Ross might get suspicious.

She'd go on this island tour with him, eking out the journey with frequent and prolonged rests. For which, of course, she would keep apologising. She might even allow herself a few angry tears at her own weakness.

She gave her pallid reflection a bracing grin, then took a deep breath and walked through to the living area.

Ross was standing at the stove, dishing omelettes on to two plates.

Macy's brows lifted as she sat down. 'Fresh bread?'

'Frozen and reheated. I run the freezer off the generator.'

'Of course,' she said. 'The simple life.'

'If by simple, you mean lacking in unnecessary complication, yes,' he retorted. 'Electricity's an essential.'

'And holding me to ransom isn't complicated?'

'Unavoidable,' he said. 'You'd hardly have accepted a direct invitation.'

'You're so right.'

He brought the plates to the table. The omelettes, she noticed bitterly, were perfect as usual, golden, succulent and moist. Like many men, Ross was impatient with housework, but a good, almost instinctive cook.

'Just like old times.' He sat down opposite her.

'Not in the slightest.' If her mouth hadn't been watering so frantically, she'd have thrown the plate at him.

'Be patient,' he said softly, cutting into the crusty loaf. 'You'll be surprised how easy it will be to turn the clock back.'

'You're wrong,' she said. 'Everything's changed. I'm not the same trusting, gullible fool I was when we first met.'

'Yet you're still involved with your father and dear old Cameron,' Ross drawled. 'Isn't that rather a contradiction in terms?'

She bit her lip. 'You've never had much time for Cameron, have you?'

'It's mutual,' he said laconically. 'No doubt the prospect of owning Thunder Cay and turning it into some glorified theme park will compensate him for missing out again with you.'

'You actually think he's that mercenary?' Her voice rose incredulously.

'Yes, I do. I always have. Your father and he had his marriage to you planned like some kind of merger years ago. And they had their sights set on this island in exactly the same way. All I had to do was drop a hint in the right quarter and they were sniffing round like rats with a piece of cheese.' He paused. 'I had to gamble they'd send you, of course. That's why I stressed negotiations had to be confidential. You've made quite a name for yourself in a quiet way. I'm impressed.'

'You really had it all sussed,' she said bitterly.

'I guessed they'd take the bait,' he returned. 'They must be getting desperate.'

'Not so desperate that they'd allow me to be part of some sordid transaction.'

'Grow up, sweetheart,' he said brusquely. 'In property circles, they reckon Cameron would sell his granny if someone offered the right price. You'd be a very small clause in a deal as potentially lucrative as Thunder Cay.'

'You're disgusting.'

Ross shrugged. 'You're not the only one who's abandoned a few illusions along the way,' he returned. 'You used me once. Now I'm repaying the compliment.'

'How dare you say that?'

'Because it's the truth. Face it.' His voice hardened. 'That's why our marriage had to be kept secret "until the right moment". That's what you kept telling me. Only there was never going to be one. I was good enough to have in your bed for a while, but not worth a lifetime commitment. Isn't that how it was?'

'Damn you,' she said unevenly. 'You walked out on me.'

'Did I have a choice?'

'I think so.' And her name was Judy Ryan, she added silently.

'We'll agree to differ on that. But now the world's moved on, and we're free to choose again.' His voice gentled, and his glance touched her like a caress. He stretched a hand to her across the table. 'Take a chance with me, Macy. I want you back in my life—back in my bed.'

The brush of his fingers was all it would take, she thought helplessly. The merest contact of skin against skin, and she would be lost for ever, drawn down into the dizzying sensual thrall he knew so well how to weave. If she took his hand, all the lonely, heated dreams would become magical reality—for a time. While she salved his damaged pride. Gave him, maybe, the child he wanted. But after that—what then? Her heart seemed to close. She clasped her hands together in her lap, forcing a cool smile.

'The world's full of willing women, Ross. Try your powers of persuasion on them instead. I'm afraid they don't work for me any more.'

His mouth twisted in a smile. 'Who said I was really trying?' he asked, and went on with his meal as if nothing had happened.

And, after a bewildered pause, Macy did the same.

In spite of her emotional turmoil, she could have eaten every scrap on his plate as well as her own, yet with superhuman control she made herself pick at her eggs, as if her appetite was still minimal.

Accordingly, she refused the sliced mangoes Ross offered for dessert, but drank two cups of strong black coffee.

'Do you feel up to this walk?' Ross gave her a searching look, as he cleared the table.

If the alternative was remaining here with him, she was fit enough to scale the north face of the Eiger, she thought grimly.

'As long as it isn't too far.' She tried a brave smile.

'It's not a very big island. But then, you know that already.' He produced the straw hat again. 'And this time you'll wear it,' he added shortly.

She didn't argue. She couldn't afford any more moments of weakness. Not genuine ones, anyway, she thought as she followed him reluctantly out into the sunlight.

Those brief moments when she had yearned to touch him had taught her succinctly that she could not trust her senses, or the physical needs he himself had taught her. She was going to need every atom of strength she possessed to keep Ross at arm's length until this nightmare ended, and she was free again.

But, a small, cold voice inside seemed to be telling her, that freedom might cost her a harsh and bitter price.

CHAPTER SEVEN

THE track from the beach led uphill. The gradient was only slight, but half-buried rocks, loose
stones and rampant undergrowth made the going
hazardous. Macy soon found she didn't have to
pretend to be breathless.

She was glad, too, of the need to concentrate.
Ross walking ahead of her was a distraction she
didn't need. She'd forgotten, or tried to, the lithe
effortless stride, the sense of male power ema-
nating from him.

'Want some help?' he asked when she hesitated at the broad bleached limb of a tree completely blocking their path.

In line with her role as semi-invalid, Macy
forced a wan smile. 'Maybe.'

His hands closed on her waist, and, shocked,
she found herself lifted bodily into the air. She
was no featherweight, but the life he'd been
leading since their separation had turned his
muscles to tempered steel.

For an endless moment she was clamped
against him, the half-naked warmth of his body
penetrating her thin clothing as if it hadn't existed
at all, making her potently aware of the clench

of muscle and sinew as he lowered her gently to the ground on the other side of the tree.

It was a stark reminder of his physicality. A disturbing warning that if he chose to use his strength against her she would be helpless. A battle of wits seemed the only recourse she had, but so far Ross had appeared able to keep ahead of the game there too.

'Thank you,' she managed, dry-mouthed. He wasn't touching her any more. He wasn't even near her, for heaven's sake, but already walking on ahead, yet the sensation of being in his arms was as vivid as if she carried the imprint of his chest and loins superimposed upon her own.

A wave of heat, which had nothing to do with the afternoon sun, swept through her. She rallied herself fiercely.

'Sorry to be so feeble,' she tossed carelessly after him.

'I should keep it cut back, but I don't come this way that often.' Ross slashed with his hand at an intrusive clump of undergrowth.

'It'll all have to be completely cleared anyway.' Macy spoke the thought aloud, and received an ironic glance.

'I'm sure it will,' he said. 'Nature can be such an inconvenience for rich people who like their playgrounds tidy.'

She bit her lip. 'We're not out to ruin the island. Just to use its natural resources to their best advantage.'

Keep to business—strictly business—she told herself as the pounding of her heart began to steady.

'You've been well-programmed, Macy,' Ross commented, his mouth twisting. 'Tell me, how did the Gilmour-Denys spies discover this place? It's been Hilliard private property for generations, and no one sets foot here without an invitation.'

'As I've discovered to my cost,' Macy muttered. 'As a matter of fact, Cameron saw it himself some years ago. He came down here and chartered a plane to look at a number of possibilities. What he saw of Thunder Cay seemed to inspire him, and as soon as he got back to Britain he commissioned plans and drawings. The whole thing became his dream.'

'And a dream with a high profit-margin,' he said softly. 'What could be better?'

'You'd know all about that, of course,' she returned evenly. 'Unfortunately for Cameron this particular dream isn't likely to come true. The cost is far too high.'

'How can you put a price on paradise? And is the decision yours to make anyway?'

'We won't argue about it,' she said shortly. 'The sooner this whole farcical situation comes to an end, the better.'

'Is that how you see my honest attempt to heal the breach between us?' he asked mockingly.

When was honesty ever part of our relationship? The question hovered unspoken on her lips. They were getting into deep water here.

She allowed her steps to falter, then stopped altogether, leaning against the trunk of a convenient tree, and fanning herself gently with her hat.

Ross stood watching her, hands on hips, a slight frown creasing his forehead.

'Are you all right.'

'Fine.' She tried a note of faintly quivering bravado. 'A route march is the best thing for anyone recovering from heatstroke.'

His frown deepened. 'We haven't much further to go. Unless you'd prefer to turn back.'

'No,' Macy said, smiling like a gallant little trouper. 'I'd much rather go on—really. What am I going to be shown—a secret cache of pirate gold that Old Bevis hid for a rainy day?'

He shook his head. 'A family treasure of a different kind.' He held out his hand. 'Come on.'

'I can manage.' She hung back. There was no way she could cope with the clasp of Ross's fingers round hers. Once they'd walked hand in hand together everywhere. For a moment she could almost smell the river mist on the Thames Embankment, feel the scuffle of dried leaves under her feet in Hyde Park.

I only had to reach out and he was there for me, she thought. Now his hand was outstretched again, and the evocation of that time of innocent happiness was too much pain to bear.

'As you wish.' He shrugged, and walked on.

After a pause, she followed, hugging her arms round her body.

The gradient had steeped perceptibly, and she kept her head down, taking each step with care. The last thing she wanted to risk was a twisted ankle.

The tangle of trees was thinning out, she realised, and ahead of them was a grassy knoll topped by an imposing house, built on two storeys. The thick stone walls were white, and the upper floor was encircled by a wrought-iron balcony.

So the beach shack wasn't the only habitation after all, Macy thought. But who occupied all this faded grandeur, which seemed so oddly familiar?

As they got closer, her throat closed with disappointment as she registered the peeling paintwork, the glassless windows, and the untended vines straggling over the walls.

'What is this place?'

'It's the original Hilliard house, built in the eighteenth century by Gervase Hilliard. He came here with a few slaves to try and establish a cotton plantation.'

'Slaves.' Macy wrinkled her nose. 'How appalling.'

'To us, yes,' Ross agreed levelly. 'To our ancestors, slavery was one of the economic facts of life. And Gervase was looking to make his fortune.'

'From cotton—here?' Macy's brows lifted.

'He wasn't the only one by any means. You'll find similar ruins throughout the islands. The Deveaux plantation on Cat Island was famous.'

'Why did he need the money?'

'He was a younger son, and he'd fallen in love with a rich man's daughter,' Ross explained. 'He grew good quality cotton, and for a while the plantation prospered. He was even able to build this house for his future wife, and when it was ready he went to Nassau to claim her.'

'And lived happily ever after? He deserved to, after all that hard work.' Macy kept her tone light.

'Alas, no,' Ross said softly. 'He arrived just in time to witness her marriage to another man— a wealthy Yankee.'

'Oh.' Macy digested this as they walked toward the bare rectangle which had once held the main door. She hoped Ross wasn't drawing any parallels. Not that there were any of course. 'Then I hope he soon found consolation.'

'No, he never did. He returned here, freed his slaves, and set fire to the cotton. He moved out of the house, too, and went to live on the beach in a kind of shelter built from palm fronds. It's supposed to be from him that the Hilliards get their capacity for solitude.' He paused. 'And possibly for falling in love with the wrong women,' he added levelly.

Macy moved hastily towards the door. 'Is it safe to go in?'

'Safe enough,' Ross said. 'And rather sad.'

She saw what he meant. In decay, the house had become a kind of conservatory. In places where the floor had rotted, shrubs grew freely, and in the former parlour, a small tree had forced its way through, its top branches reaching toward the open sky, clearly visible through the broken roof.

There was no staircase, but Macy could see the marks where it had once stood, like scars on the spotted walls of the square entrance hall.

The smell of vegetation was sharp, almost rank.

She shivered. 'Did it have to get like this? Couldn't it have been reclaimed—repaired in later years?'

'There were several unsuccessful attempts, but few people ever feel easy here. It's said Gervase still hangs around, hoping his lady will come to join him.'

'Oh.' Macy looked round, frowning. It had occurred to her why the house had seemed familiar. It was the basic design which Cameron had chosen for the central hotel block in the projected complex.

He must have glimpsed it from the plane that day—a gracious mansion crowning a hill. From that distance he wouldn't have noticed its dilapidation. But his plans for the complex were for luxury and upbeat hedonism. A resident ghost would hardly be a marketing plus for the clientele he had in mind.

'What happened to Gervase,' she asked eventually.

'He disappeared without trace one day. It was assumed that loneliness and disappointment got too much for him, and he simply walked into the sea.'

'Or maybe another boat came along, and he cut his losses, and sailed off to find another life and a new lady,' Macy said energetically.

Ross looked at her unsmilingly, 'Maybe. Is that the solution to everything, Macy—off with the old, and on with the new?'

'I try not to make sweeping judgements.' She turned towards the doorway.

'Yet you had no hesitation in judging me.' His hand descended on her shoulder, halting her, swinging her round to face him.

Colour rushed into her face. 'Stop that. I don't want...'

'I'm sure.' There was bitterness in his voice, a small flame blazing in the aquamarine eyes. 'But this is one time, Macy, when you don't get your own way.'

He pulled her against him, his hand lifting to twist in her hair, making it impossible to struggle. He said thickly, 'Don't fight me, Macy—just remember...'

For a moment, his dark face seemed to hover over her, like a hawk with its prey in sight. She tried to say, 'No' but the word emerged as a small incoherent sound. Then he swooped, his mouth closing on hers, making further protest impossible.

The heated intensity of his kiss took her by storm, the sensuous movement of his lips on hers melting her initial resistance like frost before a flame. Her lips parted helplessly to allow the more intimate access he was demanding. A slow, sweet trembling began in the pit of her stomach and spread through every fibre of her being.

This was what she had feared—had wanted so desperately to avoid. This sudden drowning in sensation—this obliteration of reason by the stark demands of her flesh.

Remember? she thought in despair, as she breathed the familiar scent of him. Oh, God, how could I forget?

His free hand lifted, encompassing one rounded breast through the thin top, his thumb moving almost hypnotically on the hardening nipple, creating a height of sensitivity that rapidly became a small agony, demanding surcease.

Whimpering silently, Macy felt herself push her hips forward, the molten core of her womanhood seeking the certainty of his erection.

'God.' The word rasped hoarsely from his taut throat. He propelled her back against the wall, crushing the ferns growing there, filling the air with their heady aroma. His hand dragged at her skirt, searching for her, all finesse—all gentleness suddenly dissipated under the driving force of a need as savage as it was mutual.

She wanted him to fill her—to make her complete—a whole woman once more. To wipe away the empty sterility of the past four years, and remember how it had been...

Remember. Suddenly all the passionate connotations of the word changed, and it rang in her head like a tocsin. Warning her. Making her realise where she was and what was happening to her. Dragging her back from the edge of the abyss.

'No.' The word tore out of her like a scream. Her hands balled into fists, belabouring furiously at his chest. Shoving him away from her, rocking him back on his heels by the suddenness of her attack. 'Leave me alone.' She dashed her hand across her mouth as if trying to wipe away the stain of his kiss.

He stared at her, dark colour along his cheekbones, his chest heaving as he dragged air into his lungs.

'Macy.' His voice cracked. 'In God's name—don't do this.'

'You started it,' she flung at him, her voice high and strained. 'No pressure. That's what you said, you bastard. I should have known I couldn't trust you.'

'I wanted you,' Ross retorted, his tone grim. 'And you wanted me. Or is that what you can't forgive, my beautiful uncaring wife? That you switched off the calculator in that icy little brain of yours and started behaving like a human being?'

There were tears perilously near the surface. But she couldn't afford to let them show. No sign of weakness. No surrender.

She said rawly, 'Damn you, Ross. Think what you like. But from now on, keep away from me.'

She turned, her head high, and walked away from him out of the empty, eyeless house, with its legacy of heartbreak and loneliness, and back down the track which led to the beach.

She'd gone about fifty yards when he came after her.

'Macy—slow down. You'll make yourself ill again careering off like this.'

'Much you care,' she said bitterly. 'It was your idea to—maroon me here.'

'If you're hoping I'll do the decent thing and let you go, you'll be disappointed.'

'Hardly. Decency has never featured very highly with you.'

'If that were true,' Ross said slowly, 'you'd be still at the house, on the floor, without your clothes, enjoying the re-consummation of our marriage.'

'Enjoying?' Macy shook her head. 'I think "enduring" would be more appropriate.'

'And "hypocrite" even more applicable.' Ross's tone bit.

Macy glared at him, and set off down the track, Ross keeping pace at her side. They maintained a frosty silence until they reached the fallen tree, which she scrambled over in undignified haste before Ross could offer his assistance. But her hurry cost her dear. As she swung herself to the ground, a protruding twig caught in her skirt and ripped a jagged tear, mid-thigh.

'Hell's bells.' Macy lifted a clenched fist to the sky. 'The only thing I have to wear and it's in rags.'

'Hardly.' Ross went on one knee to inspect the damage, and Macy recoiled.

'Just keep away from me,' she said between her teeth.

'If you can stop over-reacting for one moment,' Ross said wearily, 'there's a sewing kit at the shack. But if wearing a mended skirt offends your principles, I can offer a small selection of alternative clothes which will fit you.'

'Women's clothes?' Macy stared at him.

'As it happens,' he nodded.

Well, she didn't have to ask whose they were, Macy thought, pain commingling with anger deep within her. Naturally Judy Ryan would have stayed over on Thunder Cay—shared a meal at Ross's table—slept in his bed. The images ached on her inner vision. And the other girl was expecting to return, or she wouldn't have left a change of clothing there.

She said curtly, 'I think I'll opt for the needle and thread.'

Mouth compressed, he said, 'Just as you wish.' And this time it was his turn to walk away.

Macy followed at a resentful distance. Did he really think she'd be prepared to wear his mistress's clothes? Or did he imagine she was still unaware of the relationship?

Even if I hadn't been shown those photographs of them together in London, I'd have had to be blind and deaf to miss her performance in the hall at Trade Winds, she thought, seething.

When they arrived back at the beach house, Ross handed over the sewing kit unsmilingly.

'I'm going to catch some fish for dinner,' he said, adding with chill civility, 'Would you like to come with me?'

'Thank you, no.' Macy made a business of hunting out a spool of white thread. 'I'm going to do my mending, then have a rest,' she added, recollecting belatedly her role as semi-invalid. 'This afternoon has been tiring.'

He nodded. 'Unbridled stroppiness can have that effect.'

Macy stiffened. 'You feel I should meekly submit to being manhandled—sexually harassed?'

'On the contrary,' he returned. 'Meek submission is the last thing I want from you, darling. Start thinking in terms of unrestrained passion.'

He sent her a mocking salute, and left the shack whistling.

Macy called him a rude word under her breath, and instantly jabbed the needle into her finger. Karma, she thought wearily, sucking away the bead of blood. The sting of the tiny, insignificant wound brought the lurking tears to the surface at last, and she sank down weakly on to the edge of the sagging sofa, and wept, until she could weep no more...

She couldn't believe, she thought, pressing her fists childishly against her wet eyes, how quickly—how fatally quickly her treacherous body had succumbed to Ross's lovemaking.

She had totally failed to gauge the depth of her own sensual hunger, or the fragility of the defences she could mount against him.

And he had let her go. That was the humiliating truth she now had to live with.

Because if he'd ignored her objections—mastered her protests—taken her in his arms again, she would have given herself with total, unreasoning abandon. And the realisation stunned her.

She shivered, tucking her legs protectively under her, and huddling into the cushions. She found herself thinking with a kind of panic, 'Where can I go? What can I do?'

She became aware of the scent almost at once, faint, elusive, and exotic as it tantalised her nostrils. She bent to sniff at the cushion, and as she did so caught sight of something white half-hidden down the side of the sofa.

She tugged it free. It was a woman's handkerchief, in good quality white linen, monogrammed with the single initial 'J'. The scent too was stronger, and quite unmistakable. 'Ysatis' she thought almost reflectively, as her fingers convulsively crushed the scrap of material into a tiny ball. The fragrance Judy Ryan had been wearing at Trade Winds.

Proof of the other girl's recent presence on the island, if proof were needed.

With a quiver of revulsion, she dropped the crumpled ball of material on to the floor.

What cruel game was Ross playing? she asked herself wretchedly. Why couldn't he be content with the woman who'd been his intimate companion for the past four years or more, instead of trying to force an unwilling wife back into his arms on his own outrageous terms.

Hurt pride, she thought wearily, or revenge. That was the only explanation. And no relationship could be built on such treacherous foundations.

'You used me once,' he'd told her. 'Now I'm repaying the compliment.'

It was as simple as that. And no amount of passion could ever make it acceptable.

Her head had started to ache again. She would go into the other room, she thought. Stretch out on the bed, and try and gain some oblivion in sleep.

She could only pray that this time there would be no heated, sensuous dreams to torment her.

She got up slowly, pushing her hair back from her tear-streaked face, staring ahead of her with pain-filled eyes. Life without Ross had been a desert of emptiness. But to live with him again, knowing she was merely being used, would break her heart.

She took a deep, steadying breath, then bent and retrieved Judy Ryan's handkerchief from the floor, stuffing it into the pocket of her torn skirt.

Another woman's scent, she told herself, to serve as a constant and potent reminder that Ross was another woman's man.

CHAPTER EIGHT

MACY must have slept, in spite of her emotional turmoil, because, when she opened her eyes, the room was filled with the strong rosy glow of sunset.

She became aware of other things too. A faint crackling noise, allied to a scent of woodsmoke, and another more savoury smell which made her mouth water suddenly.

And, also, that a thin blanket had been placed over her while she slept on top of the bed.

She bit her lip. It was an act of kindness on Ross's part, that was undeniable. But the knowledge that he'd been in the room while she was asleep and vulnerable was disturbing.

His room, she thought, looking round her. His bed.

She was thankful that she'd taken the trouble to shower away the marks of pain and distress, and mended the rent in her skirt before she took her rest. She'd have hated him to find her tearstained and unkempt. She needed every scrap of self-possession and respect she could get.

She got up, smoothing the creases out of the much-tried white skirt, then went outside on to the small veranda.

A little way down the beach, Ross was kneeling beside a driftwood fire, above which, impaled on sticks, two fish were cooking. He was tending them, his expression intent, absorbed. Then, as if aware of her regard, he turned his head and smiled at her.

For a second, the years, and all else that had served to distance them, fell away, and she felt her heart lurch, suddenly and painfully. Be careful, she adjured herself, as she walked down the steps and began to cross the sand towards him.

'I hope you don't object to a barbecue,' he said as she reached his side.

'Not at all. Don't you ever get bored with this Robinson Crusoe act of yours.' Her voice was unnecessarily tart.

'Not yet,' Ross said cheerfully. 'Don't you get fed up with the rat race—even if you are involved with some of the chief rats?'

'Very funny,' she said stormily. 'However, I prefer their company to some I could mention.' She took a breath. 'Ross, isn't it time we called a stop to all this? I think you've amused yourself long enough at my expense, and now I'm getting annoyed.'

Ross gave her a laconic look. 'I'm sure the minions at Gilmour-Denys may jump when you snap your fingers, darling, but I don't. Go practise being imperious somewhere else.'

'Unfortunately, at the moment, there is nowhere else,' she snarled. 'I'm asking you to send for the boat to take me off.'

'But the honeymoon's hardly begun, my sweet. And there's a lot more of the island to show you.'

'A pleasure I'd prefer to forgo.' She sank down on to one knee beside him. 'Ross, I'll make a deal with you.'

'That's what we're here for.'

'No.' She swallowed. 'Not that kind of deal. Let me go, now, and I won't say a word about what's happened to anyone. The last thing your father needs—or mine—is some monumental scandal.'

'What's so scandalous about a husband and wife reconciling under a tropic moon? All the world's supposed to love a lover, Macy.'

'We are not,' she said, 'lovers.'

'Not yet.'

'Not ever. We both have new lives—new relationships.'

His mouth twisted sardonically. 'Cameron Denys is hardly that. He's been there, waiting for your father to hand you over, gift-wrapped, since the day you left school. But Thunder Cay should be sufficient compensation.'

She said, 'I intend to tell the Gilmour-Denys board that it was all a mistake—that Thunder Cay was never for sale.'

He shook his head. 'Too late, darling. Ambrose Delancey will have told them by now

that negotiations are under way.' He paused.
'Although not, of course, the actual form they're
taking.'

He examined the grilling fish, nodded with
satisfaction, and served them on to plates.

'Madam's dinner is served.' He pointed to a
rug spread on the sand. 'Take a seat.'

Macy took the plate he handed her, and with
one, sweeping gesture, tipped the fish back into
the flames.

Ross watched its cremation without expression. 'You should have said you preferred it
well done,' he remarked eventually, stretching out
on the rug, and pulling a tray set with cutlery,
glasses, and bottle of wine on ice towards him.

He uncorked the wine, filled both glasses, and
began to eat with every evidence of enjoyment.

Macy watched sullenly. That had to be one of
the most meaningless gestures of her life, she
thought. And she was starving.

'Here.' Ross held out a glass of wine to her.
'Or have you decided on total abstinence as well?'

It was a Californian vintage she particularly
liked, dry, but with a strong fruit base. There
seemed little point in cutting her nose off a second
time, so she sipped in inimical silence while Ross
finished his meal.

Daylight was only a pale flush of memory in
the sky, and the moon was climbing, golden and
benign above the palm trees. The breeze that

came from the sea was still warm, but Macy found she was shivering just the same.

'Cold?' he asked.

'No.' She was silent for a moment, feeling the wine caress her throat, and tingle through her veins. Then she said huskily, 'What do you want me to do, Ross? Go on my knees—beg you for mercy?'

'When you beg,' he said slowly, 'it certainly won't be for mercy. And it will be in my own good time, not yours. I've waited four years for you, so I can hold back till you decide to drop the pretence—and I don't mean your imitation of the Dying Swan this afternoon,' he added, with curt derision.

Macy flushed defensively, 'I didn't ask to get heatstroke...'

'To hell with that. I'm talking about a more fundamental dishonesty.'

'I don't know what you mean.' She stiffened.

'No? Then I'll be happy to give a brief demonstration.' He put down his glass and leaned over, detaching hers from her suddenly nerveless fingers.

'Ross...' Fright, and some less easily identified emotion, tightened her throat.

'Hush,' he said. 'It's all right. I'll make it all right.'

He moved beside, pressing her down without force on to the rug. Then his head and shoulders blotted out the moon, just as his kiss blotted out thought and reason.

This time, he was almost frighteningly gentle, allowing his lips and tongue to play with hers, until the taut rigidity of her mouth trembled into compliance. And as the moist, sensuous invasion continued, she felt a sigh of pleasure quiver through her body.

His lips placed a trail of tiny kisses along her jaw, and down the curve of her arched throat, finding every pulse, every sensitive area of delight.

He took the edge of the silken top between his teeth and tugged at it gently. She could feel the warmth of his breath through the thin fabric. Could feel her nipples firming in response, even before he bent and let his lips close round each tumescent peak in turn, laving them with his tongue through the clinging material.

Her arms lifted, almost of their own volition, to lock behind his head, and hold him to her. Later, she thought dazedly, she would hate herself for this. But now—ah, God—now...

With a stifled moan, she arched her whole body in offering—in surrender.

But Ross was moving too—rolling away from her, his breathing suddenly harsh.

She looked up startled, and saw him get to his feet.

'Ross.' It was a little cracked whisper. 'Don't leave me—please...'

In the gathering darkness, he was a tall shadow standing over her, but his voice had a cool and ruthless clarity.

'It wasn't so hard to make you beg, after all, Macy. But I'm afraid the demonstration's over for tonight. I said it would be brief.' He paused. 'Sleep well. I give you my word you won't be disturbed.'

He turned and walked away down the beach towards the silver ripple of the sea.

'Fool. Idiot. Imbecile.'

Macy muttered the words as she sat on the sofa, staring sightlessly ahead of her.

So much for self-control, and all her good intentions. Without even trying, Ross had entangled her in a fleeting web of tender sensuality.

The tenderness, of course, had been her undoing, coupled with the sheer drenching sweetness of familiarity which had overwhelmed her in those charged moments up at the Hilliard house.

Ross's mouth, she thought achingly. Ross's hands.

Her need for him had simply been dormant. Her mind might deny him, but her body knew better.

What's the matter with me? she asked herself wretchedly. What kind of woman could still want a man who cynically and cold-bloodedly walked out on her for money? A man, who now only wanted her back for his own selfish and devious purposes.

A woman in love, of course. It was that simple. That fundamental.

Even if she was able to escape from Thunder Cay tomorrow, she would love him all her life. She could admit that now—acknowledge it in the deepest part of her soul. Not even the shame and heartbreak of his rejection had been able to change the way she felt about him.

The life she'd rebuilt had been a sham—a flimsy façade dragged together to shield her from self-knowledge.

One thing was certain. No matter how she might long for him, and for the fulfilment she would only ever know with him, she couldn't allow the bond of a child to tie her to a man who'd treated her with such heartless contempt.

Our child should have been conceived in love, she thought sadly. Not as a matter of expedience, or as compensation for imagined wrongs. After all, I was the one who was wronged.

Macy looked at the curtained entrance to the bedroom, her mouth tightening. His parting words had seemed to imply she could go to bed in safety tonight. But she knew the danger had never been more real. Not from Ross, but from her own weakness—her own desperate yearning.

She bit her lip, and focused her attention on the closed door next to the bedroom. Presumably it led to another room of sorts, but even if it was little more than a glorified cupboard she reckoned there'd be enough floor space to make up a bed for herself with the sofa cushions, and a blanket.

Unless, of course, it was locked. But to her relief, when she tried the heavy wooden handle, it turned easily, and the door opened towards her, with a faint squeak from its substantial hinges.

And inside was a compact and comprehensively equipped dark room.

Macy's brows snapped together. She supposed she should have guessed. He'd made no secret of the fact that he was still continuing his photographic career, and he'd said electricity was an essential.

The room didn't seem to be in use at the moment, although she noticed the radio he'd mentioned tucked into a corner. Her lips tightened. She knew nothing about sending transmissions, but she might have to do a crash course if all else failed.

There were several bulky folders on one of the work units, and Macy picked up the top one and opened it.

For a moment, she thought she was looking at some mysterious enchanted garden. Then she realised that the strange misshapen branches she saw were of coral, and the vivid splashes of gold, rust and orange weren't clumps of flowers at all, but sponges.

It was a wild, alluring underwater world confronting her, she realised with amazement.

She carried the folder back to the sofa, and leafed through the prints with mounting excitement.

Ross hadn't concentrated solely on coral, with its towering halls and bottomless caverns. There were detailed studies of other forms of marine life too. She recognised the exotic parrot fish, and the more homely grouper, as well as a shoal of angel fish.

And there were other, more sinister shapes, too. A moray eel, spotted like a leopard, and a hammerhead shark, with its distinctive blunted snout, and long streamlined body, dwarfing the girl diver, who swam below it like a miniaturised shadow.

She was in several of the shots, her hair streaming around her head like a blonde nimbus, and quite unmistakable.

Macy thought, Judy Ryan, and bit her lip till she tasted blood.

'Seen enough?' Ross's voice sounded harshly from the doorway.

Macy had been too absorbed to be aware of his approach. She started violently, but managed to retain her hold on the folder, as she got to her feet.

'I'm sorry,' she said awkwardly. 'I didn't mean to pry.' She forced a smile. 'I should have guessed why that door had to fit so well.'

'Probably.' He held out his hand for the folder, but she hesitated.

'They're very good. Did you take them locally?'

He nodded. 'Most of them off this island, and Fortuna. But we went down to the Abacos as well.'

Did we indeed? thought Macy. She indicated the photograph of the shark with its human counterpart. 'That took some guts.' She tried to keep her tone admiring, but impersonal.

'It isn't quite as hazardous as it seems. Sharks rarely bother divers unless provoked in some way. And Cliff Ryan was handling the security side of things, as always.'

'Cliff Ryan?' Macy's brows rose interrogatively as she relinquished the folder.

'Judy's brother. He runs a diving school and underwater exploration outfit on New Providence. He wouldn't let anything happen to either of us. Besides, Judy's very experienced. She was practically born in the water.'

'Yet she chose nursing instead.'

Ross nodded. 'She trained at one of the big teaching hospitals in London.'

So that's what she was doing there, thought Macy.

'When she qualified, she decided to come back to the Bahamas to do private nursing,' Ross went on. 'Her diving, these days, is purely recreational.' He paused. 'And, of course, she's very decorative.' His tone was bland. 'She photographs well, even in a wet suit, and as she works at Trade Winds she's always on hand.'

'Yes.' Macy put a hand in her pocket, and touched the tight ball of Judy Ryan's handkerchief. Always on hand. Always available.

She tried to smile. 'Are the photographs for a magazine spread—the *National Geographic* or something?'

Ross shook his head. 'They're for a book,' he said. 'The breakdown of coral is getting to be a serious environmental issue these days, and I was commissioned to write and take pictures about the life and death of a reef. The proceeds will be used for experimental work to try and halt the decline.'

'Being Ross Hilliard has its advantages,' she said.

He shrugged. 'Actually I was first offered the commission four years ago, when I was still relatively unknown.'

And when you were still with me, she thought numbly. So that was where you vanished to—sailing and diving in the Bahamas with your lady and her brother.

It could also explain why Ross had taken her father's money so readily. She wasn't sure what kind of publishing advance such a book could command, but if it was intended for an environmental charity it was unlikely to be high. Ross would have needed additional finance for his research.

She smiled resolutely, 'So you finally got to do what you wanted—make a record of one of the world's last wildernesses. Congratulations.'

'It was certainly fascinating,' he said quietly. 'The adventure of a lifetime.'

The lifetime that we planned, she thought in anguish. The adventure you promised me. Oh, Ross...

He frowned slightly, his eyes raking her face. 'You look tired,' he said abruptly. 'Go to bed.'

He took in the sudden hectic flush along her cheekbones, the desperate clenching of her hands, and his expression gentled slightly. 'Macy, I said you were safe tonight, and I meant it. Go and get some rest.'

He turned towards the stove. 'I'm going to make some coffee before I turn in. Do you want some, or does it still keep you awake?'

Her heart ached at the accuracy of his memory. She said stiltedly, 'It—still does.'

'Need anything else?'

Only your arms around me. The words seemed to clamour in her head.

'No,' she said brightly. Maybe too brightly. 'No, thanks. Not a thing.'

She walked into the bedroom, and let the curtain fall into place behind her.

She could hear the sound of thunder in the distance. Macy grimaced, and turned up the collar of her trenchcoat. Storms always made her nervous. She hoped she'd get back to the flat before this one broke.

Perhaps it was the build-up in the weather which had made her edgy all day. Or maybe she was just looking forward to being home with Ross.

Things had been strained between them before she left.

'Do you have to spend the weekend at your father's?' he demanded.

'He's got a delegation of Japanese businessmen to entertain, Ross,' she tried to explain. 'He needs me.'

'I need you,' he said sombrely. 'Macy, you're my wife, not your father's tame hostess, and it's time he was told.'

'Yes,' she said. 'Yes, I know. But not yet. I want to get him accustomed to the idea, slowly.'

He said flatly, 'I don't think there'll be enough time in eternity for that. We should have told him right away, and to hell with the consequences.' He framed her face in his hands. 'There are things we need to discuss this weekend—important things.'

'That all sounds very dire,' she said lightly. 'But I have to go down to Caldecott. There's some paperwork to do with the Landin Trust I have to deal with as well. Won't your important things keep until Monday?'

He was silent for a moment, then he shrugged. 'It seems they'll have to,' he said, and kissed her.

It had been an odd weekend. Her father had seemed preoccupied, as if he was only going through the motions of being a genial host. Yet he was usually in his element, disguising business as pleasure at Caldecott Manor.

Nevertheless, a highly successful deal had been struck on Sunday morning, and by the time their visitors departed that evening Macy had been dropping with weariness, mingled with celebratory champagne.

She tried hard to listen attentively to Sir Edwin's painstaking explanations of the Trust documents she had to deal with, and had dutifully scribbled her signature where indicated, before crawling thankfully up to bed.

She usually had a lift with her father after these weekends, but to her astonishment when she woke on Monday morning, she found he'd left an hour earlier than usual. And then the housekeeper took advantage of her presence to bring a whole catalogue of queries to her attention—the kind of domestic trivia that Sir Edwin never heeded.

Accordingly it was lunchtime before she could get away and catch her train. And although she'd attempted to phone Ross several times to warn him she was going to be late, there was no reply from the flat.

Perhaps he'd been offered an assignment, she thought hopefully. They'd been thin on the ground lately, although she'd assured her father that everything was wonderful. She felt guilty each time she did so, knowing the secret she was harbouring. Perhaps Ross was right, and she should simply tell her father she'd been a wife for six months rather than wait for some ideal moment that might never come.

The front door of the flat was open, and she flew in, calling, 'I'm back. Have you missed me?' then stopped, because it wasn't Ross waiting in the living-room, but her father.

She checked, disconcerted. 'Daddy?'

After all, it was the first time he'd set foot in the place, and he looked grave, and rather pale, as if he found his presence there distasteful.

She thought, he knows—he's found out about the wedding.

He said heavily, 'You'd better sit down, my dear. I have some—bad news for you.'

He seemed to recede to a great distance. She heard herself saying very calmly and distinctly, 'There's been an accident, hasn't there and Ross is dead.'

'No,' Sir Edwin said bitterly. 'He's very much alive, or he was when I spoke to him earlier.'

'You and Ross have been together?' Macy moved bewilderedly to switch on a lamp. The sky was dark as slate outside.

'He came to the office by appointment,' Sir Edwin confirmed. 'He had what he called—a business proposition to put to me.'

She laughed. 'But Ross doesn't know anything about big business. He's a photographer.'

'Is he?' Sir Edwin said grimly. 'I'd say fortune-hunter and confidence trickster might be more accurate descriptions.'

'How dare you?' Blood burned in Macy's face. 'You've never even tried to like him—or to understand why I love him.'

'Do you blame me? When he stood in front of me only a few hours ago, and asked me how much I'd be prepared to pay him to get out of your life once and for all? He said he knew he'd never be acceptable in your world, and that your relationship wasn't working. However, he couldn't afford to just—fade out of the picture.' Her father's voice rose angrily. 'That's the man you love, Macy. A common shyster.'

She was very still. 'No,' she said. 'It can't be true. There must be some mistake.'

'Macy.' Her father took her icy hands, chafing them. 'I know what you must be feeling, how terrible this must seem. But believe me, it's all for the best. Illegitimate—penniless—living by his wits.' He snorted with contempt. 'Sweetheart, you're well rid of him.'

'He's gone?' Her reeling brain tried to make sense of what was happening. As if on cue, lightning flashed, to be followed almost at once by a long, low rumble of thunder. 'You—paid him to go.'

'It was what he wanted.' Sir Edwin spoke in a low, urgent voice. 'He must have had this planned from the start—from the moment he discovered who you were. He knew that I'd be thankful to get him out of your life, so he stayed just long enough to push the price up.'

'I see.' Her voice sounded like a stranger's. 'And exactly how much am I worth—in current market terms?'

'You'd better see this.' He took a folded paper from inside his coat, and handed it to her.

It was quite a simple document. It stated that, for the sum of one hundred and fifty thousand pounds, the undersigned, Ross Bannister, forfeited all claims, either financial or personal, on Macy Landin Gilmour.

The signature was unmistakably Ross's—an angry slash across the page, under the words 'Received with thanks.'

Another flash of lightning. Thunder—like the crack of some kind of doom.

Macy stared down at the paper. Macy Landin Gilmour, she thought. Not Macy Bannister. Nausea, bitter as gall, rose in her throat. She said, 'Is this all. He didn't say anything else about me—about our relationship?'

'No.' Sir Edwin stared at her, paling. 'Macy— you don't mean—surely there isn't a child on the way?'

She said quietly, 'No that isn't what I mean. I was wondering if he offered any explanation.'

There was a silence, then he said, 'There is an explanation. I hoped I wouldn't have to hurt you with it.'

Photographs—spilling across a table. She pushed them away and ran to the bedroom.

Ross's half of the wardrobe was bare; the drawers in the tallboy were empty; his suitcases had gone.

When the thunder roared again, Macy put her hands over her ears, and started to scream.

CHAPTER NINE

MACY sat bolt upright in bed, her heart hammering. Another dream, she thought dazedly. And its cause was not far to seek. Somewhere in the reaches of the night, there was a low, persistent growl of thunder.

She pressed her hand over her ears to blot out the sound, stifling the instinctive moan of distress which rose in her throat. Storms had this effect on her now. They brought back nightmares she wanted to remain buried in her unconscious mind forever.

She felt very hot. She hadn't undressed before she lay down, and her clothes were sticking to her clammy body. By morning, they'd be unwearable.

But at the time anything had seemed better than lying naked in Ross's bed, waiting for him to come to her.

In spite of his assurances, she was sure he would continue to sleep with her, as he'd done when she was ill, and the prospect of that dangerous proximity made her throat tighten in panic.

Only she was alone.

The thunder was still rumbling, steadily and monotonously, and although the sound was faint, it was there, and it made her feel as if she was stifling—choking in this room. She had to get out—to breathe—to regain her equilibrium.

Ross was fast asleep on the sofa. In the moonlight, through the open door, the curve of his bronzed body was clearly outlined under the single sheet that he'd partly kicked away. Macy looked down at the width of his shoulders, the long, graceful line of his back, the smooth turn of his hip, and felt her mouth grow dry.

There was a time when she'd have woken him at a time like this, she thought. When she'd have asked for comfort, for reassurance, her fingers featherlight against his spine, her mouth pressing kisses on to his cool skin.

And even still half drugged with sleep he'd have turned to her, smiling, and pulled her into his arms, sheltering her with his body.

But that was long ago.

Tensely, she began to edge to the door, her eyes fixed on him, but he didn't stir, even when a floorboard creaked under her foot.

Outside, the breeze from the sea was stronger than it had been during the day, and Macy drew several deep, grateful breaths. She ran a hand round the nape of her neck, lifting the heavy fall of her hair away from her skin, easing her shoulders irritably beneath the clinging, sticky top. A shower would be ideal, she thought longingly, but she couldn't risk waking Ross.

The alternative, of course, was a swim. The gentle splash of the sea on the beach sounded beguiling, and she walked down the sand, shedding her clothes as she went.

The last few yards were wonderful, untrammelled and free. She'd often heard that skinny-dipping was the only way to bathe, she thought, as she waded out into the lagoon, but this was the first time she'd tried it.

The water felt cool and sharp on her heated skin, and when it reached mid-thigh level she lowered herself into it completely, with a little gasp of pleasurable shock.

She swam for a few yards, then turned on her back and floated, the water lapping her like silk.

The sea by night was full of movement, sound and colour undreamed of in daylight, she discovered, as long slow ripples lifted her, then let her subside gently.

The distant thunder was louder now, but she could see no flashes of lightning in the sky, only the gleam of spray along the reef, and a hint of phosphorescence in the calmer water of the lagoon.

And, nearer at hand, a steady splashing growing louder.

Macy turned her head to discover the source, and found Ross suddenly, startlingly, beside her.

Her body jack-knifed in shock, and she swallowed a mouthful of sea and choked.

'Are you crazy—suicidal?' Even muffled by the water in her ears, his voice sounded molten with rage. 'Get out of here, now.'

'You're the one who's mad,' Macy flung at him, coughing, as he began to assist her none too gently towards the shore. 'The storm woke me, and I just wanted to cool off.'

'Storm?' Ross dumped her on the beach. 'What bloody storm?'

'Can't you hear the thunder?' She scrubbed at her stinging eyes. 'I hate thunder.'

He listened for a moment, then laughed harshly. 'That's no storm. It's the sea breaking on the reef. It makes that noise when the wind freshens and veers slightly. That's how this place got its name—Thunder Cay.'

'The reef?' she repeated. 'Is that all it was?'

'It's enough,' he said drily. 'Don't underestimate it, especially in a boat.' He paused to shake some of the water out of his hair. 'Now, listen, Macy. You don't swim at night off this island, or any other. Nor do you ever swim alone. You could get into difficulties.'

'I'm not a helpless child,' she said with dignity. 'Actually, I'm quite a strong swimmer.'

'You,' he said grimly, 'are not alone in that respect.'

He took her by the shoulders, turning her, and pointing towards the reef, where those brief trails of phosphorescent light still glimmered.

'That's the wake of a big fish—probably more than one,' he said. 'Sometimes sharks come inshore at night looking for food.'

'Oh,' was all she could think of to say. Suddenly the velvet night had turned on her. It was full of danger, and a chill that penetrated to her bones, and her teeth were chattering.

In fact, she was trembling all over, but that wasn't because of the menace she'd unwittingly invited. She was suddenly, desperately conscious of her nakedness and his.

'I'm cold.' She tried to conceal the shake in her voice.

Ross muttered something rough and exasperated under his breath, then pulled her to him, and, before she could say or do anything to prevent it, he'd lifted her up in his arms as easily as if she'd been a child. Holding her, he began to walk back up the beach towards the shack.

'My clothes...' she began, but he shook his head.

'We'll look for them tomorrow. Let's get you warm and dry first.'

She let herself relax into the strength of his embrace, as the warmth of his body communicated itself to hers.

She should not be allowing this, a small voice in her head warned. But, dear God, it was good to be this close to him again. To feel safe—secure in his arms—even if that was an illusion.

Reality would return with the dawn, and she would face it then.

She turned her head, and buried her face in the curve between his throat and shoulder, feeling the strong pulse throb against her probing lips. She touched her tongue to his skin, licking away the salt. Reminding herself deliriously of the warm male essence which belonged to him alone. She was savouring him, anticipating all that was to come as she pressed herself against his bare chest, feeling her nipples peak in delicious excitement at the contact with his hair-roughened skin.

It was Ross's turn to shiver. 'Macy.' His voice was raw. 'For God's sake . . .'

He carried her straight into the bedroom, lowering her on to the bed, and detaching her clinging hands.

'Get under the covers.' His voice was strained. 'I'll make you a hot drink—something with rum in it.'

'No,' she said, watching him through half-closed lids. She reached out and touched him gently—recklessly. Stroked her hand down the flat plane of his hip. Let it linger. Watched his body's instinctive, involuntary response to her caress, and smiled. This time he would not find it so easy to walk away.

The bed was as soft as a pillow, and she was a siren, luring him to his doom and ultimately—

inevitably to her own as well. Only, she didn't care any more.

Nothing mattered. Only this night, and the two of them together again. Reunited after the long, barren years. Her need for him was as deep and elemental as the ocean itself.

Her voice was soft. 'Stay with me, Ross. Warm me. It's been cold for so long.'

Ross sighed, a harsh sound of capitulation.

'Too cold,' he muttered. 'And four endless years too long. Oh, God, Macy...'

He lay beside her, reaching for her, and she went into his arms as if she'd never been away. Their bodies moulded together in an aching, wrenching silence which spoke more loudly than any words. Their mouths touched, tentatively, questioningly at first, then with a burgeoning fierceness and certainty.

Ross's mouth began to explore her body, feathering across her breasts, before drawing the proud nipples into his mouth. The movement of his tongue across the aroused peaks sent desire, jagged as lightning, exploding across her nerve-endings.

Again, she could hear the thunder on the reef, but it was closer now, all around her, pounding in her pulses, echoing through her veins.

His thigh grazed hers, and she lifted herself against him in swift urgency, letting her body speak for her, making its own imperative demands. Showing him that she was more—more than ready for the culmination.

Ross threw his head back, a groan of acceptance escaping his taut throat. He entered her in one strong, fluid movement, and her body melted in welcome for him, closing around him, replying moistly and heatedly to each slow, lingering thrust.

Ross, she thought dizzily, had always made love as if there was all the time in the world. And nothing had changed. He would make this last to the edge of eternity—and beyond...

Her hands clung to his sweat-slicked shoulders. His damp chest hair rasped against her sensitised breasts, lancing them with a pleasure akin to pain.

Her slender legs enclosed him, drawing him deeper, holding him inside her forever. The rhythms of love, which he himself had taught her, lifted and dropped them like the ebb and flow of the sea lapping the shore only yards away from them.

She was the moon that drew the tide, and he was the high golden sun that flamed and glittered in every fibre of her being. Who gave her new substance and meaning in the shadows of her universe.

The slow, deep drive of his body into hers possessed her, controlled her totally, and she focused almost blindly on each new and intense sensation breaking over her.

Even so, the first dark spasms of rapture took her unawares. Then, utterly consumed, her body convulsed and shuddered against him—around him in the sweet violence of her release.

Macy heard herself cry out hoarsely at the beauty and power of it, and felt sudden grateful tears scald on her cheeks.

Ross's hands framed her face tenderly. He kissed her mouth, then licked the drops of salt away from her skin and lashes, waiting for the dizzying spiral of delight to abate.

Her return to earth was slow. Out of her languid, delicious euphoria, she tried to speak—to say his name, but he shook his head, placing a silencing finger on her parted lips.

Then, very gently, the union between them unbroken, he turned on to his back, holding her astride him.

Hands on her hips, he held her still for a moment like some creamy statue of a pagan goddess, a faint smile playing about his lips as he studied her.

Macy lifted her hands, flicking the sea-damp strands of mahogany hair back from her shoulders and breasts, watching the sudden flare in his eyes as she did so.

He began to touch her, running his hands easily and fluently over the planes and contours of her body. His fingers teased a pattern from the base of her scalp, down to the nape of her neck, then followed the delicate line of her back, questing, with a faint frown, her too-prominent shoulder-blades, tracing each vertebra as if it was precious to him. His hands stroked down to her flanks, making her arch sensuously, as he rediscovered her. Enjoyed her.

She was smiling too, now, pursuing an exact path through the mat of hair on his chest with her fingertips, seeking the flat male nipples, making them stiffen and pucker under her touch, before she bent to brush them with the tips of her own breasts. Listening to the change in his breathing. Watching the aquamarine eyes blaze into hers like blue diamonds. Feeling him stir within her, telling her silently that he had waited long enough.

Now, it was her turn to make love to him, and she did so, moving slowly, sensually, erotically against him, her whole body attuned to his pleasure, obeying each intimate, unspoken signal, as they led each other once more into the warm labyrinth of passion, seeking the dark, secret core of ecstasy at its heart.

But this was for him—all for him, she told herself languorously, swaying backwards a little, cupping her breasts enticingly, smoothing her fingers down over her body to her thighs, and the dark, silky triangle at their apex.

Knowing that for him, watching her was part of the delight. Taking him gradually, inexorably to the knife-edge of release, then holding back.

Tantalising him. Delaying the moment when his world would splinter into exaltation.

But when that moment came, when she heard him cry out, his eyes glazed and unseeing in sublimation, when she felt him erupt like a flame inside her—then, to her astonishment, she found her own body clenched and quivering under its own new shock-wave of fulfilment.

'That was greedy of me.' Aeons, light years later, she murmured the words into his sweat-slicked shoulder.

'You were starving.' She felt his lips touch her hair, like a benediction. Then, cradled in his arms, Macy slept.

It was broad daylight when she woke, and she was alone. She lay quietly for a while, letting her mind drift back over the events of the night, in a kind of elated incredulity.

She had slept in Ross's arms for a while, then awoken to his kisses, turning to him in drowsy delight as they made love again, softly and tenderly.

No dream this time, she thought, stretching pleasurably. Just golden, glorious reality.

Except for one thing. She pondered it, frowning a little, her tongue soothing her faintly swollen lips. There'd been something missing—something not quite right...

Of course, she thought, suddenly. The words. 'My love. My sweet love.' He didn't say the words.

And now he wasn't here.

It was a troublous realisation, or maybe just part of the tender melancholy which so often followed lovemaking.

She sat up determinedly. She wasn't going to lie here getting the blues. She was going to get on with the day.

The first day, perhaps, of the rest of their lives.

As she pushed the sheet back, she saw the pile of clothing stacked neatly on the end of the bed.

For a moment, she was motionless. Then slowly, stiffly, she began to turn the garments over. Underwear in crisp broderie anglaise. A pair of brief white shorts. A vest top, the colour of honey. Pretty, practical, and in pristine condition, she had to admit.

But not hers. Never hers.

Macy sank her teeth into her lip, as shock gave way to growing anger.

Presumably, as she'd slept with him—made love with him in the bed he shared with his mistress, Ross assumed she would have no compunction about borrowing Judy Ryan's clothes either.

She turned to the tallboy, dragging open the drawers until she found the ones she wanted.

There was plenty of choice, she realised, feeling sick. Everything from the latest beach and leisurewear to nightgowns and peignoirs like drifts of thistledown. A world of pleasure and seduction, wrapped in tissue.

Macy slammed the drawers shut again. Her whole body was cringing as if she'd turned over a stone, and found unnamed horrors scuttling underneath. As if she'd been slapped in the face.

But she couldn't say she hadn't been warned.

She sat down on the edge of the bed, wrapping her arms protectively round herself to stop the trembling. The hurt, like a stone inside her.

Oh, God, she whispered, her throat aching. What a fool I've been. What a blind, gullible fool.

She'd let her body betray her, deliver her bound and gagged into Ross's hands. In one night, he'd achieved everything he'd set out to do when he brought her here, she realised feverishly. She'd given herself to him, passionately and completely, but with no guarantees in return.

Ross wanted a figurehead in his life. A suitable wife at his side. A mother for his child. Those were the terms he'd laid down. The deal that was on the table.

But she—she wanted so much more.

She wanted Ross as the man she'd fallen in love with—the man she'd married, with such hope. But that was the dream. The reality was the unprincipled stranger who'd taken her father's bribe, and walked out on her. The man who'd used her cynically for his own behests, and who now offered nothing but the bleak façade of a marriage, while he pursued his own pleasures elsewhere.

Well, she could not—would not accept that, she told herself starkly. She could not exist in a relationship without love or trust, no matter how sexually beguiling.

And Ross only had to crook his little finger to bring her, quivering into his arms, she reminded herself with shame.

He must think she was such a pushover that she'd be prepared to settle for whatever crumbs of a liaison she could get.

But he was wrong. Whatever the personal cost to herself, the agony of another separation, she deserved better than second-best.

The water in the shower was cool, and she used it liberally, like a ritual cleansing, washing away the taste and touch of him.

Then she wrapped the towel round herself like a sarong, and set off down the beach to find her own clothes.

The sun still had some hours to reach its full power, but it was warm enough, nevertheless, to encourage Macy, after a brief hesitation, to discard the clammy folds of towelling altogether.

Eve after all, she thought, her mouth curling ironically. Eve, who'd tasted the forbidden fruit, and then been turned out of paradise forever.

And Ross, undeniably, came under the heading of forbidden fruit. Something she should have remembered last night. Instead, she'd practically thrown herself at him, given away her true feelings with every kiss, every caress.

And now she had to face the consequences.

Her hand touched her abdomen, delicately, questioningly, as it occurred to her what one of those consequences might be.

She lifted her chin. She would deal with that if and when she had to.

She found her bra and pants, then picked her designer top out of the sand and studied it ruefully. It would be like wearing a cheese grater, but what choice did she have?

She pulled on the top, and wriggled uncomfortably into her maltreated skirt. As she tugged up the zip, a prickle of awareness shivered down her spine, and she looked up to see Ross coming down the beach towards her.

He was covered minimally by another pair of disreputable shorts, and had a camera slung over his shoulder.

In spite of everything, Macy felt her heart lurch crazily and hopelessly.

'I left you some things. Didn't they fit?' There was no trace of last night's shared warmth and intimacy in the cool eyes that observed her. No particular triumph either.

'I wouldn't know.' She kept her voice equally impersonal. 'I prefer my own clothes.'

He said, after a pause, 'I see.' He turned away, and began to walk back towards the shack. 'I'm about to make some coffee,' he tossed over his shoulder. 'Unless you have qualms about accepting that too.'

He was actually behaving as if she was being unreasonable, Macy realised, seething as she followed.

She said shortly, 'It's hardly the same thing.'

'Oh?' Ross shrugged. 'I'm afraid your methods of discrimination are beyond me.'

I could say the same, she thought tautly, as he filled the kettle and set it on the stove.

'Anyway,' he went on, 'you won't have to wear those things much longer.' He fetched beakers, spooned granules into them, his attention concentrated on the task. 'I've sent for the boat. You're leaving—going back to Fortuna.'

She was leaning against the table. Behind her back, her fingers curled round the hard, wooden edge, gripping it until her knuckles turned white.

'What's made you decide that?' Her voice sounded as if it was coming from a distance.

He didn't look at her. 'Macy, don't let's pretend.' His voice was weary. 'I was wrong and I admit it. Our marriage won't work. It can't. Not without commitment and that doesn't exist. Maybe it never did.'

He swung round. The aquamarine eyes blazed at her. 'I should never have done this. It was madness, but it's not too late to salvage the situation. I'll take your offer—a quick divorce. Serve the papers, and I'll sign them.'

He threw his head back. She saw the veins taut in his throat. 'Only make it soon,' he added curtly. 'I want this finished—over with, at last.' He brushed past her, and went out of the door, his long stride carrying him swiftly out of sight.

Out of her life for good, she thought numbly.

Yet that was what she wanted, she told herself rigidly. What had to be. And she should be thankful for it.

So, why was the desolation inside her enough to fill the world?

CHAPTER TEN

MACY sat on the floor in the parlour of the old Hilliard house, her back against the trunk of the little tree, staring sightlessly up through the broken roof at the sky.

She wasn't sure why she'd come here—except that it seemed like a refuge from the shack, and all its recent memories. Or, maybe, a place serving as a monument to a love affair that had gone wrong just suited her present mood, she thought wryly.

She'd waited half an hour for Ross to return, but there'd been no sign of him. She made the coffee when the kettle boiled, and threw it away cold and untasted.

Unhappily restive, she'd begun to prowl ridiculously up and down the beach before calling herself sternly to order. If she needed exercise she'd take a proper walk, she decided, and instinctively her steps had turned towards the track up to the house.

She looked around her with a sigh, wondering idly how much it would cost to restore the house to a habitable condition. Even in its present sad state, it had an undeniable charm. And it was a

Hilliard family heirloom, however little that might concern her.

The house needed attention, she thought wistfully. It needed filling with love and laughter, and the rough and tumble of family life.

She lifted a hand, and patted the slender tree trunk behind her. 'I wouldn't cut you down,' she said. 'You'd be a feature.'

But it wasn't up to her, and never would be.

What she had to consider instead was what she would say when she got back to London, what explanations she could offer her father—and Cameron—about the failure of the deal.

The first thing she would have to reveal was the truth about her marriage. That it had existed. That it was now over—completely and finally.

Ross's words of rejection still seemed to be beating in her brain.

For the second time, he'd closed her out of his life and walked away, but this time no one had needed to pay him to do it. It was his own free choice, she thought, pain lancing through her.

Was this how Gervase Hilliard had felt when he returned here alone? she wondered. Had his life seemed a total desert, without happiness or even hope?

But she wouldn't become a recluse as he had done. For this time she might have something from the wreckage to console her.

But even if that crazy, ecstatic night had not given her Ross's child, her life would still change.

She intended to resign from Gilmour-Denys, and become completely independent. If the Landin Trust couldn't provide enough to occupy her time, she might start some kind of business. Maybe even restoring old houses.

She got to her feet, dusting off her clothes. A token gesture, she supposed, considering the state of them, then paused to pick a small spray of leaves from the tree.

Something to keep, she thought. To remind her always, as if she needed any such prompting.

As she emerged from the front door, she saw Ross striding up the slope towards her. He halted abruptly when he saw her, his face set.

'What the hell are you doing here?'

'Just saying goodbye.' Macy lifted a shoulder. 'I hope that's permitted.'

'Of course.' For a moment, his usual incisiveness seemed to have left him. 'It's just—I didn't expect—I didn't know where you'd gone.'

'Not very far,' she said. 'Now this is a really small island.'

His smile was wintry. 'Yes.' He paused. 'The boat is almost here.'

The hours had gone, she thought. All she was left with now were minutes—even seconds. And they were ticking away.

She said quietly, 'I'll come at once.'

She collected her bag from the shack, and walked down to the jetty where Ross was waiting, watching Sam manoeuvre *Sweet Bird* alongside.

And not alone either. Macy's steps faltered as she recognised a blonde head, surmounting a tanned body, provocatively displayed in a vivid blue halter top and clinging knee-length pants to match.

Judy Ryan—come no doubt to gloat over the spoils, she thought grimly.

From some undreamed of vat of courage she dredged up a smile, pinning it resolutely in place.

'Well, hello.' Judy's smile was cat-like as she jumped ashore. 'I thought I'd come along for the ride.' She looked Macy over critically as Ross, having greeted her quietly, began an low-voiced conversation with Sam. 'How's the recovery going? You still look rather—worn.'

'I'm fine, thanks,' Macy responded coolly. 'But I'll be glad to go home. I don't think the local climate suits me.'

'Actually you weren't all that ill,' Judy said. 'But like most men, Ross is inclined to panic a little.' She paused. 'I suppose he felt partly responsible for your being sick—having virtually kidnapped you.'

Macy looked at her levelly. 'I see there aren't many secrets at Trade Winds.'

Judy gave a little laugh. 'Well, it is a very close-knit household.' She paused again. 'And I do rather have a vested interest in Ross.'

'So I gather.' Macy forced herself to speak calmly, when in reality she wanted to scratch her nails down the other's smug face.

'I wasn't very happy about his seeing you again,' Judy went on. 'I tried to warn him against it. But apparently it was something he needed to do—like a kind of exorcism, maybe.'

'Really?' Macy gritted her teeth. 'Well, if you're expecting my head to spin round, or for me to vomit live toads, you're going to be disappointed.'

'Oh, I don't think so.' Judy's eyes were limpid with satisfaction. 'In a way, I suppose I should be grateful to you—if it means that Ross is going to finish with his past, and give up being a hermit on this damned island for ninety per cent of the time. Maybe life can become normal at last.'

'You don't like Thunder Cay?' Macy ignored the implications in the other girl's words.

Judy's brows lifted. 'What is there to like about the back end of nowhere? A creepy old house in the middle of a few acres of nothing.' She gave a little artificial shudder. 'I hope your company does make something of it. We could do with some upbeat life round here.'

'I don't think that's likely to happen.'

'No? I presumed that was why your father had arrived at Trade Winds—to finalise the deal.'

Macy stared at her. 'My father?' she repeated dazedly. 'What do you mean?'

'Ross hasn't told you that he turned up earlier?' Judy shrugged. 'Perhaps he was keeping it as a pleasant surprise.'

Macy felt hollow inside. A confrontation with her father was the last thing she needed. She'd hoped for a breathing space—some kind of brief respite to pull her life—her future together.

She said, quietly, 'No doubt,' and turned away.

Ross came over to her, his expression set. He said, 'You've heard you have a visitor?'

'Yes.' Macy shook her head in bewilderment. 'I can't think what he's doing here.'

Ross's swift smile was sardonic. 'He's come to find out what's happened to his precious deal,' he said. 'Not to mention his precious daughter.' He paused. 'I think I'll forgo the pleasure of a reunion with him.'

'I quite understand.'

'Now that,' he said, 'I doubt.' He took an envelope from the pocket of his shorts and gave it to her. 'A farewell gift.' His voice was suddenly harsh. 'To remind you of old times.'

'I don't need that...' she began.

'Take it anyway,' Ross said.

Macy made a business of pushing the envelope into her shoulder-bag. She didn't want to watch Ross walk away with Judy Ryan. It was not a final image she needed—the pair of them on Thunder Cay—together. But that was undoubtedly what the other girl had in mind.

Sam helped her on board *Sweet Bird*, his expansive smile slightly subdued. She took a seat in the bows, looking ahead of her.

As the boat moved off, she heard Judy laugh, softly but with a note of rising excitement.

It might as well have been a fanfare of victory.

Macy stared at the horizon—at the future—and found her vision oddly blurred. And frighteningly bleak.

Unlike most return journeys, it seemed endless. Sunk in her bitter thoughts, Macy forgot about Ross's envelope until they were nearly back at Fortuna.

She took it listlessly out of her bag. There was no message of greeting or explanation on the envelope. Just her name. A farewell gift. So, it was neither an apology or a love letter. But then, Ross had never been good at either of them, she recognised achingly. She was sorely tempted to throw it overboard, and let the wind and sea carry it away forever.

But curiosity triumphed in the end. As she opened the envelope, one swift glance told her what the contents were—a cheque drawn on a major London bank, and made out to Ross Bannister for one hundred and fifty thousand pounds.

Macy stared down at it in mingled incredulity and disbelief.

She thought, He kept it all this time without cashing it. But why? It makes no sense—no sense at all. To take a payment of this size, but never use it . . .

She swallowed. So he hadn't left her for money after all. That had just been an excuse. The real reason had been her inability to hold him—and his lack of commitment to her.

That, of course, was why he'd decided to let her go now. Because he didn't care enough, and never had. Never would. Because he'd been honest enough to recognise that a mere physical rapport was not sufficient basis for a lifetime's marriage.

Because he now had the woman he wanted, and was not prepared to settle for a convenient second-best either.

Macy sighed, and thrust the cheque, still in its envelope, back into her bag.

In a way, it was a relief to know that Ross's motivation hadn't been completely mercenary. On the other hand, it also served to deepen her feelings of hurt and rejection even further.

As Macy walked into Trade Winds, she met Ambrose Delancey coming down the stairs.

'Mrs Hilliard.' His greeting held a certain reserve.

Macy winced slightly. 'I don't think it's really appropriate to call me that any more,' she said quietly.

'No. Ross's message indicated the hoped-for *rapprochement* had not taken place.' His tone was kinder. 'It was not a course of action I advocated, of course. But he seemed to feel the situation called for desperate measures.'

'Yes.' Macy forced stiff lips into a smile. 'But I want you to know, Mr Delancey, that I won't make any waves—over anything. The important thing is for us both to be legally free, as soon as possible. Especially as there's someone else involved,' she added stiltedly.

'So I gather.' He nodded towards a door across the hall. 'You're aware that your father is waiting for you. He's in rather an agitated state.' He paused. 'Mr Hilliard senior's health doesn't permit him to have house guests, unfortunately, but I've been able to get an additional reservation at your own hotel.'

Macy shook her head. 'Thank you, but we'll be returning to the UK right away.'

'I hardly think so. Sir Edwin wants the Thunder Cay deal finalising before he leaves, and it will take a few days to draw up the necessary papers.'

Macy stared at him. 'You mean Ross is going ahead with the sale?' she asked incredulously.

Mr Delancey nodded. 'He radioed his instructions a short while ago.'

It hadn't taken Judy Ryan long to make her influence felt, Macey thought sadly. She forced a smile. 'In that case, I'll be flying home alone.' She held out her hand. 'Goodbye, Mr Delancey.'

'Good luck, Miss Gilmour. A car is at your disposal whenever you choose to return to Fortuna Town.'

'Thank you.' Clearly the sooner they left, the better, she thought drily. She lifted her chin. 'It's been—quite an experience.'

And it's not over yet, she added silently, as she prepared to face her father.

Sir Edwin was prowling restlessly round a large room, furnished predominantly in white. He was an incongruous even sombre figure in his dark suit. As Macy entered, he swung round, his brows snapping together as he surveyed her.

'My dearest child.' He sounded appalled. 'You look terrible. I've been beside myself.'

'Hello, Father.' Macy crossed the room, and kissed him on the cheek. 'I'm fine,' she went on carefully. 'What are you doing here?'

'I was informed that you'd been deliberately stranded on Thunder Cay with Ross Bannister.' His voice shook. 'Naturally, I came at once to put a stop to this outrage—to rescue you.'

Macy sighed. She could, she thought, make an educated guess as to his informant's identity. 'There was really no need,' she said, quietly. 'As you can see, I'm fine.'

'Fine?' Sir Edwin was scandalised. 'Macy— you can't have seen yourself. You're in rags. You look like some down-and-out.'

'Nevertheless, it's true,' she said firmly. 'And—yes, I have been with Ross, but that's all over and finished with. There was no need for you to be involved.'

'Involved?' Sir Edwin echoed shakily. 'Are you mad? When that swine walks back into your life—has the gall to abduct you...'

Macy hunched a shoulder. 'He wanted us to have some privacy to discuss a possible reconciliation.' She tried to keep her voice matter-of-fact. 'But in the end, we agreed it wouldn't work.'

'I should think not.' Her father looked as if he'd been poleaxed. 'How dare that blackguard have the unmitigated gall to pester you again? Or does his supposed relationship to Boniface Hilliard set him outside the bounds of decent behaviour?'

Macy bit her lip. 'Well, at least he can't be accused of being after my money, this time,' she said wearily. 'Not that it matters. The fact remains that he still doesn't want me.'

'My poor sweet,' Sir Edwin said heavily. 'I shall never forgive myself for sending you here—subjecting you to this ordeal. Cameron, of course, is quite distraught.' He patted Macy's shoulder. 'As soon as you've got over all this—recovered your looks, we'll announce your engagement.'

'No,' Macy said forcefully. 'We will not. Not now. Not ever.'

'Macy.' Sir Edwin gave her a minatory look. 'You're upset. You don't know what you're saying. Believe me, my dear, I know what's best

for you. You need loving care, my dear, a stabil-
ising influence in your life.' He smiled coaxingly
at her rigid face. 'And you must see that
Cameron's long devotion should be rewarded.'

'On the contrary,' Macy said flatly. 'I've never
even considered marrying Cameron. I don't care
for him, and I've not encouraged his so-called
devotion.' She took a deep breath. 'In fact, I
think it would be best—less embarrassing all
round if I resigned from Gilmour-Denys when
we get home.'

'No.' If her father's face had been florid before,
it was ashen now. 'Macy—you can't do that.'

'Why not? I'm a free agent.' Or I will be very
soon, she added silently, with a pang of anguish.

'Because you're going to marry Cameron,' he
said energetically. 'It's always been an accepted
thing. And he's been more than patient waiting
for you to get over this—absurd infatuation.'

'Has he?' Macy lifted her brows. 'Well, that's
unfortunate. Is Cameron also prepared to accept
that my—infatuation could have repercussions?'

There was a silence. Sir Edwin was looking at
her as if he'd never seen her before. 'Macy,' he
said hoarsely. 'You don't—you can't mean...'
He stopped. 'Oh, God.'

Macy said steadily. 'It's a possibility, but I
didn't intend to break it to you like this. Let's go
back to the hotel. We can talk there while I pack.'

Her father didn't seem to have heard her. 'My
poor child,' he said, shaking his head. 'That it

should come to this.' He squared his shoulders. 'But you mustn't worry. Everything can be taken care of. No young woman has to ruin her life these days.'

Macy stiffened. 'Stop right there. This is your own potential grandchild that you're talking about.'

'No.' His voice rose to a shout. 'I won't accept that. I can't. I won't allow you to give birth to an illegitimate child—bring shame on our family, after all my hopes—the plans I've made for you?' He drew a shuddering breath, trying to regain control. 'Dear God, I thought I'd got Ross Bannister out of your life forever. Now, you could be having his bastard. Are you quite mad?'

'If I am pregnant,' she countered quietly, 'I shall indeed be a single parent. But the baby won't be illegitimate.' She took a breath. 'There'll never be a right time to tell you this, Father. Ross was quite right about that.' She threw back her head. 'He and I are married.'

'You've married him?' Sir Edwin looked suddenly grey and old. 'Here—on Fortuna?'

Macy shook her head. 'No,' she said gently. 'Four and a half years ago—before he pretended to take the money and run.'

He sank down on the edge of a snowy-white sofa. 'No.' He sounded almost piteous. 'It can't be true.'

Macy sat beside him. 'I never intended you to know,' she confessed. 'I'd planned a discreet divorce after five years' separation. But Ross had—other ideas,' she added with difficulty.

'Oh, yes.' The look her father sent her was almost manic. 'I suppose this is his idea of revenge. Of destroying me. And you, little fool, played right into his hands.'

Macy bowed her head. 'I can't deny that. But you won't be destroyed. Whether I'm pregnant or not, I'll move right away—out of London. Make my own life. You really don't have to worry.'

'Worry.' Her father's short laugh was harsh. 'My God, Macy, you don't know the half of it.'

'Well, at least you're going to get Thunder Cay.' She put her hand over his, but he shook it off.

'It will take more than that to save me now,' he muttered. 'My God, Macy, do you know what you've done?'

She said bitterly, 'I'm beginning to.' She got to her feet. 'We can't stay here, Father. We'll go back to the hotel, have a rest and talk again.' She forced an encouraging smile. 'Try and sort something out.' She paused. 'Give me a minute to arrange our transport.'

She went out of the room, closing the door behind her, then went quietly and quickly up the broad staircase to Boniface Hilliard's room.

She tapped on the door and entered before she could have second thoughts.

'So, it's you.' He was occupying his couch by the window, his face brooding. 'I thought you'd have been out of here by now.'

'I'm sure you did,' she returned levelly. 'But I wanted to say goodbye.'

'So, you've said it.' There was no softening in the pale eyes which were so like Ross's. 'I wasn't in favour of Ross's crazy idea to win you round, Miss Gilmour—or Landin or whatever you choose to call yourself. But when he sets his mind on something, it's hard to turn him round.'

'Yes.'

'When I found him, he was in a hell of a state,' he said harshly. 'I see no reason to forgive you for that, even if he can.'

'It was Ross who walked out on me.' Macy's eyes flashed. 'What about my feelings?'

'If you'd loved him, you'd have wanted to share his life. But you weren't prepared to give up a thing for his sake. What man—what real man is going to be his wife's lap-dog, dancing to her tune all the time?'

'You think I wanted that?' Macy shook her head. 'I'd have gone anywhere with him.'

'As long as it was five-star accommodation, and first-class travel all the way.' The blue eyes glinted fiercely at her. 'You should have hung on for a week or two, young woman. It might have made a difference.'

Macy shook her head, the image of Judy Ryan vivid in her mind. 'I don't think so,' she said huskily.

'That's what I thought.' Contempt rang in his voice. 'Did he give you the cheque back? He planned to.'

'Yes.' Macy was silent for a moment. 'If he didn't want the money, why didn't he just—tear it up?'

He smiled grimly. 'He wanted it as a souvenir. A permanent reminder of the biggest mistake he ever made in his life. If he's handed it back, I hope that means he's ready to start living again.'

She said quietly, 'I think his new life started a long time ago, Mr Hilliard. And I hope your new daughter-in-law is more to your taste. Goodbye to you.'

She would not cry, she vowed as she went downstairs. She would not give him that satisfaction.

But as Sam started the car that would take her away from Trade Winds forever, she was weeping inwardly.

And in her aching head, she seemed once again to hear the distant sound of thunder on the reef.

CHAPTER ELEVEN

IT WAS going to be a very long day.

Macy delivered her father to the bungalow adjoining hers at the hotel, adjuring him to rest. Then, in the privacy of her own room, she stripped off her clothes, throwing them into the waste bin in the bathroom. She would ask the maid to burn them, she thought, as she stepped under the shower.

She dried herself, pulling on one of the hotel's towelling robes, then stretched out on the bed, looking up at the ceiling fan as it slowly revolved.

This room—in fact, everything on Fortuna—only served to remind her of Ross, she realised bleakly. Four years had not been enough to effect a cure. How long, this time, would it take her to heal from the wound he'd made?

If she closed her eyes, he seemed to be imprinted on her eyelids. If she turned her face into the pillow, it seemed redolent of the warm male scent of him.

Imagination, she thought, was a dangerous thing.

The cool shower had refreshed her. It had also made her hungry. She reached for the bedside phone, and rang room service for a double order of coffee and club sandwiches.

'Is that instead of the bottle of whisky, Miz Gilmour?' came the cheerful query, and Macy bit her lip, as she realised who that must be meant for.

'No, as well as, please,' she said constrainedly.

She replaced the receiver and stood for a moment, frowning.

Sir Edwin had sat in a brooding silence throughout the car journey, his face haggard and like a stranger's. The last thing he needed was to drink himself into oblivion as she suspected he intended. On the other hand, a couple of snorts to relax him would do little harm.

In a way she was tempted to join him—try and find an alcohol-induced oblivion from pain and emotional hunger. But there were decisions to take and plans to be made, and she needed a clear head.

She swung herself off the bed, and dressed swiftly in cream cotton trousers, and a raspberry-pink top.

The first essential, of course, she thought, as she brushed her hair, was to get away from Fortuna altogether, and all its disturbing associations. With the finality of air miles between them, maybe she could begin to heal. And as soon as she got back, she would consult a doctor at an advisory clinic, and find out how soon a pregnancy test could be conducted. Her entire future, after all, hinged on the result, although she was aware life could never be the same again, regardless of whether the test was positive or negative.

As to where she would live, she supposed the world was her oyster. Except, of course, for the one place she really wanted to be.

When her food order arrived, she went next door and persuaded a patently reluctant Sir Edwin to join her on her terrace.

He drank some coffee, but only picked at his food, giving jet lag as an excuse, but Macy wasn't convinced.

She said gently, 'I'm going to ask Reception to call the airport for me, Father. You don't need me for the Thunder Cay negotiations, so I'm flying back.

His mouth tightened. 'No doubt your former husband will make us pay over the odds.'

'I hope not,' Macy said evenly. 'However, I don't think Ross will fail to cash your cheque this time around.'

Her father's cup clattered back into its saucer. 'What are you talking about?'

Macy sighed. 'The money you paid him four years ago,' she said. 'He never used it. He just kept the cheque with him all this time—as some kind of symbol of female perfidy, according to his father. Although why...' She stopped. 'Dad— are you all right?'

'It's the heat,' he said. He produced his handkerchief and wiped his forehead. 'I'm not used to it. He kept that cheque, you say?'

'Yes, until today.'

'Did he show it to you?'

'More than that—he gave it to me as a souvenir.' Macy gave a wintry little smile.

'That was very cruel.' Her father's voice shook. 'As if you needed any reminder of that terrible period in your life, or the way he treated you— betrayed you.' He held out his hand. 'Give me the cheque, darling, and I'll destroy it. You can't want to have a thing like that around you.'

'I'll get rid of it in my own good time.' Macy patted the bag hanging from the arm of her chair. 'It could prove a salutary lesson.' Then she frowned. 'But, dad, you must have known this all along. You must have realised the money hadn't left your account.'

'But naturally, I thought—I assumed...' He sounded totally at a loss. 'I didn't actually verify the transaction.'

What a word, Macy thought sadly, to describe the destruction of her marriage. The death of all her hopes and faith.

Her father was speaking again. 'I don't blame you for wanting to get out of this place, darling. I'll phone Cameron and ask him to meet you from the airport.'

'No.' Macy shook her head forcefully. 'I really don't want that.'

'Macy.' Sir Edwin leaned forward, his brow furrowed. 'This last week has unsettled you. I understand that. But when you get back to London, you'll feel differently, I'm sure.'

'If you mean my feelings for Cameron may change, Father, then you couldn't be more wrong,' she said gravely. 'I don't love him, I never have, and I never will. It's as simple as that.'

'That's the problem.' He was perspiring heavily again. 'I have certain commitments—certain guarantees...'

'Involving Cameron?' Macy found herself remembering some of the things Ross had said. She leaned back in her chair, with a small sigh. 'I'm sorry if you're in some kind of fix, but your arrangements with your partner are your own problem. I'm severing all connection with Gilmour-Denys, remember?'

'How could I forget.' His eyes were fixed on her urgently. 'Macy, Cameron's always wanted you.'

'I'm sorry it can't be mutual.' Her tone sharpened. 'What are you getting at.'

He dabbed at his mouth. 'I'm under a tremendous obligation to him, Macy. You could—help...'

There was a loaded silence.

She said slowly, 'I don't think I believe what I'm hearing. Are you intending I should be— some kind of pay-off for Cameron Denys?'

'I wouldn't put it as crudely as that.'

'I would,' she said grimly. 'Just how far has this gone, Father? What have you done to me?'

'Macy, I didn't have a choice. I've been in too deep for years. And now Cameron is putting pressure on. This Thunder Cay deal is only part of it.'

'My God,' she said quietly. 'Let's have the whole truth, shall we? Ross never asked you for money to get out of my life, did he? It was all your idea, to leave the way clear for the charming Mr Denys. Isn't that the case?'

'Macy.' His face was agonised.

'My own father,' she said. 'You deliberately set out to manipulate—to ruin my life.'

'Ross Bannister was never right for you,' he defended himself. 'I wanted to save you from unhappiness.'

'You wanted to save me for Cameron,' she came back at him. 'Because what Cameron wants, he must have, even if he wants to change it—remodel it like Thunder Cay.' She gave a small mirthless laugh. 'How was I supposed to turn out, I wonder?'

Sir Edwin sagged back in his chair. 'Macy.' His voice pleaded. 'You must help me. Cameron could finish me.'

'No.' She shook her head gently but firmly. 'You've got yourself into this mess, Father, but you're not taking me down with you.'

'I don't recognise you any more,' he muttered. 'What's happened to you?'

'They call it desperation.' She nodded towards the adjoining bungalow as the telephone began to shrill. 'I think you're wanted. And please don't tell Cameron I'm his for the asking,' she added icily. 'Because I wouldn't want to call you a liar as well as a fraud.'

As soon as he'd disappeared indoors, Macy snatched up her bag and headed for the car rental desk in the hotel foyer. She had no chance of getting on a flight that evening, she reasoned, so she might as well fill the remaining time by seeing the rest of Fortuna while she had the chance. After all, she would never be coming back.

This time, she headed north, putting as much distance between Trade Winds and its offshore island as she could.

She parked the car by the sea, and sat watching the faint creaming of the surf, remembering another crescent of silver sand. In her mind's eye, she saw a tall figure, lean and tanned, aquamarine eyes narrowed against the sun, his mouth curving in tender laughter. His hands gentle as he reached for her...

Oh, God, she thought unevenly. How can I bear it?

She had been shaken to the depth of her being by Sir Edwin's admission of his machinations. I never guessed, she berated herself. I never even questioned what he was telling me.

Yet what difference would it really have made? Ross hadn't come to her and told her what was going on, and that certainly wasn't because he held her father in affection or esteem. Or because he wanted to shelter her from the knowledge of Sir Edwin's deviousness.

He must have wanted out of the relationship. That was the only answer. Although it didn't explain why he'd been so bitter about the money he'd been offered. Or why he'd kept the cheque untouched.

She sighed. Perhaps there were some things she was fated never to know, she thought, trying to be philosophical. And she would do herself no good by endlessly chewing them over.

She had loved two men in her life, she thought drearily. Her father, and Ross. And she'd learned the hard way that she couldn't trust either of them. End of story.

She drove steadily, looking without seeing at the winding coast. And when evening came, she found a shoreside restaurant specialising in conch dishes, and ate there.

When she finally returned to the hotel, her father's bungalow was in darkness. She could only feel relieved. She didn't want to be badgered about Cameron, or to lose any more respect for her father by hearing further evidence of his wheeling and dealing.

She read for a while, then went to bed. But she couldn't sleep, or perhaps she was afraid to.

Afraid of what dreams might come in the night, she thought wryly, twisting restlessly on the mattress. Last night, her wildest fantasies had become glorious reality, and now her re-awakened flesh was once more greedy for fulfilment. From now on her subconscious longings would have an added edge to them.

She pulled on her robe and went out on to the moonlit veranda, moving quietly so as not to disturb her father next door. She stood for a while, leaning on the rail, absorbing the sounds and scents of the darkness. Listening to the distant splash of the sea. Remembering how, only a few nights ago, she had wanted to follow the silver path of the moon down to the beach, and find Ross waiting for her there.

Madness, as she'd told herself at the time, but such sweet madness. And this time she didn't even try to resist, although she knew Ross would not be there. He was on Thunder Cay with Judy Ryan.

It's a stroll, she tried to placate herself, as she descended the shallow steps. Just a stroll to relax me. Some fresh air. That's all.

She moved without hurrying, breathing the fragrance in the air, pushing her way past the intrusive bushes and shrubs which lined the path and caught at her robe, showering her with pollen.

At last she emerged from the sheltering palms on to the sand, listening for the thunder on the reef, but hearing only the heavy beat of her own sad heart.

In the silver moonlight, the man's dark figure was clearly visible. He stood, his back towards her, at the edge of the sea.

For a moment she was motionless, then she began to run, her bare feet sliding in the sand. She made no sound, but he turned instantly, as if alerted by some sixth sense to her presence.

They met halfway. Ross said huskily, 'Oh, my love. My sweet love.' His arms went round her, lifting her almost off her feet, as he kissed her with a deep and hungry passion.

'It's you. It's really you.' Half laughing, half crying, Macy touched his hair, his face, his chest through the half-unbuttoned shirt. 'I thought I was dreaming. What are you doing here?'

'I came to find you. To ask you to come back to me.' His voice was unsteady too. 'I was getting up the courage to walk up to your bungalow—to beg you on my knees if necessary.'

'You want me?' She lifted eyes wide with questioning to his face. 'But you can't—it isn't possible...'

Ross framed her face in his hands, his gaze tender but intense. 'I won't ask you for a lifetime commitment, Macy. You may not be ready for that. Perhaps you never will be, but that's a risk I'll have to take.'

He drew a deep, shaken breath. 'Come back to me on your own terms. If it only lasts weeks or months, then I'll survive it somehow. I'd rather have crumbs than no bread at all.'

'What crumbs?' Her arms went round him, hugging him fiercely in reply.

'Macy, don't fool with me,' he said huskily. 'You did it to me four years ago—kissed me and smiled, then flung me to the wolves.'

'No.' She shook her head. 'I love you, Ross. I've always loved you. When you left me the first time, I died a little. Today, when you sent me away, I felt as if I was bleeding to death.'

'That was self-preservation.' His voice was raw. 'I thought I'd enjoy making you suffer. The thought had obsessed me since you threw me out. I swore I'd never let you get to me again. That I'd use you next time. But the longer we were together, the more I realised I couldn't do it. Whatever had happened in the past, this time I wanted your love, and nothing else would do.'

'I didn't throw you away,' she said in a low voice. 'It was my father. He told me everything today—how he wanted to split us up so that I could marry Cameron. He fooled both of us...'

'I know that,' Ross said quietly. 'But he didn't have to succeed, Macy. If you'd stood up to him—told him we were married, for a start—fought for me, we could have won. But you just obeyed orders and consigned me to hell. And that's what I thought I couldn't forgive. Your betrayal.'

'He was waiting for me at the flat,' she said. 'He said you'd asked for money, and showed me a receipt. I was devastated—destroyed.'

Ross sighed. 'Darling,' he said. 'If we're going to have a prayer this time around, we've got to be totally honest with each other. No more pretence. And you knew exactly what was going on, my love. You had to know. It was your money, for God's sake. That's what finished me—what drove me away. Your signature on the cheque.'

For a moment, she stood like a statue in his arms. Then she said, 'No, that's not true—not possible.'

'No more games, Macy.' His voice was imploring. 'Do you think I'm blind—or illiterate? Why do you think I kept the bloody cheque all this time—to be a thorn in my flesh, and keep my anger burning.'

'You think I'm capable of that,' she said slowly. 'And yet you still came here tonight?'

'Yes,' Ross said sombrely. 'Whatever kind of a fool that makes me. I was no saint, Macy. Our marriage wasn't perfect. Maybe you had your reasons for doing what you did. If it had been your father's money, I'd have torn the bloody cheque up in his face. I'd probably have torn him to shreds too. But when I realised you were selling me out, nothing seemed to matter any more.'

'I swear it's not true,' she said. 'There must be some terrible mistake.'

'Didn't you recognise your own signature?' he asked gravely.

She started. 'I never got that far. When I realised what it was, I felt sick. I just shoved it back in the envelope.'

'Where is it now?'

'In my bag, back at the bungalow.'

'Then we'll go and find it—get to the bottom of all this once and for all.'

She'd left the bungalow in darkness, but as they approached the veranda, Macy saw a lamp had been lit in the living area.

She tensed. 'Oh, God, I didn't lock the door. Someone's in there. We'd better call security.'

'No.' Ross halted her quietly. 'I think we can handle this ourselves.'

Something in his tone chilled her. She said, 'I don't think I want to.'

'We have no choice.' He opened the door, and ushered her gently into the room ahead of him.

Sir Edwin whirled round. 'Macy?' He swallowed. 'Hello, my dear. I was looking for you. Wanted to have a word. We should never let bad feelings fester overnight, eh?'

His voice was over-loud; too hearty.

Macy stared at him, a hand at her throat. She said, 'Father, what are you doing with my bag? Did you want something from it?'

She saw his face crumple. Watched the bag drop from his hand as if it had stung him suddenly. Ross's envelope slid out on to the floor, and Macy bent to retrieve it.

Ross had followed her silently in.

Edwin Gilmour's gaze went past his daughter, and focused on his son-in-law. He said, 'You. Oh, dear God.'

Ross went over to the fridge and extracted a miniature brandy, which he poured into a glass and handed to the older man, motioning him towards a chair.

He said coolly, 'I think you have some explaining to do, Sir Edwin.'

Macy looked down at the cheque in her hand. Traced her own unmistakable signature with the tip of her nail.

She looked at her father. 'How did you trick me into signing this?' She was surprised how calm and unfazed she sounded.

'I put it among the trust documents that afternoon at Caldecott. I banked on your being too tired to look at things too closely, and anyway, I left it blank. I pointed out the dotted line, and you signed.'

'Because I trusted you.' Her voice cracked. 'Dad, how could you?'

'I had to do it. He'd never have taken money from me, but your signature was the clincher. It cut the ground from under him.' He put the glass down. 'I told him you were tired of playing house—of camping in a flat one remove from a slum. I said you wanted your old life back, but didn't know how to tell him. I said you didn't want him to leave empty-handed, but at the same time you had to be sure he wouldn't come back for more. That you'd never be content with the lifestyle he had to offer.'

'You were very convincing,' Ross said flatly.

'The money came from the Landin Trust, of course. I was going to explain the discrepancy as a number of donations to charity. But you never asked, and I presumed it had been overlooked somehow. I never dreamed that he would just keep the cheque.'

'If I hadn't,' Ross said in a voice like ice, 'Macy and I would have stayed at cross purposes all our lives. Each of us believing we'd been betrayed by the other.'

Sir Edwin nodded. 'I counted on that.'

'How could you?' Macy whispered. 'You took four years of our lives away from us.'

'But I wasn't completely to blame. He was having an affair, Macy.' Sir Edwin pointed a shaking hand at Ross. 'You saw the evidence.'

'What the hell are you talking about?' Ross demanded contemptuously.

Macy was very pale. 'Photographs,' she said. 'Of you and Judy Ryan—together in London.'

'We met a few times, yes,' he said, frowning. 'Boniface had managed to trace me, but I wasn't sure I wanted to know. I wasn't convinced that I could handle such a fundamental change in my life, so he asked Judy to make some preliminary approaches. Persuade me to meet him at least.' He touched Macy's cheek gently. 'That's what I wanted to discuss with you that weekend.'

'But she's in love with you,' Macy protested. 'She came to Thunder Cay this afternoon to be with you.'

'That's news to me on both counts,' Ross said drily. 'I think she's quite in love with becoming a Hilliard. She made quite a play for Boniface himself at one time, and it amused him to point her in my direction instead. But he knew she hadn't a chance.'

'That's not what she thought,' Macy said. 'Besides, Ross, I saw her in your arms in the hall at Trade Winds.'

His grin was frankly sheepish. 'That's what I was hoping. I heard you on the stairs, and wondered what a spot of healthy jealousy might do.' He paused. 'But I didn't ask her to Thunder Cay today, or invite her to stay. That was all her own idea—and one that she now regrets. So much so, that my father will have to look for a new nurse.'

'You sent her away?' Macy gasped.

'She fired herself,' Ross said. 'I simply made it clear I didn't need consolation of any kind, and that if necessary I was going to spend the rest of my life winning my wife back to me.'

'That isn't very fair on her.'

'No,' Ross admitted. 'But there's nothing fair in love—or war. And sometimes non-combatants get hurt—if they interfere. She'll make out.'

There was a silence. Then Sir Edwin looked at Macy.

'You're going with him?' His voice was defeated.

'Yes,' she said. 'Wherever that takes us.'

He nodded, then rose from his chair, and walked to the door. He hesitated for a moment, looking at them as if they were both strangers.

He said, 'I'm sorry,' and went out.

Ross sighed, and some of the tension vanished from his shoulders. He said, 'I wish I could have spared you that.'

'It was horrible,' she admitted quietly. 'But necessary. Honesty can't be selective.'

'And now I've got to ask your forgiveness,' he said steadily. 'For misjudging you—for hurting you.'

'We're both guilty of that,' she said. 'But we were set up by experts, and we were no match for them.'

'And now?'

Macy walked smiling into his arms. 'I could take on the world,' she told him softly, then hesitated. 'Starting, I suppose with your father. He doesn't like me, Ross. And now I've caused him to lose his nurse as well.'

'Oh, I think he'll come round,' he said. 'When I told him earlier that I was coming after you—that I wanted you at any price, he ordered me to be gentle with you. He said you had wounded eyes.'

'Oh.' Macy swallowed, feeling the prick of tears behind her eyelids. 'I thought he wanted you to divorce me and marry Judy.'

'Never in this world.' He shook his head. 'Judy was a good enough nurse, and an excellent diver, but the most I ever felt for her was gratitude.'

'But those clothes in the drawer in the bedroom—the underwear. They had to belong to someone.'

'They belonged to you.' Ross was rueful. 'Every single item, bought specially for our reunion. The trousseau, my love, you never had the first time around. And you rejected it,' he added in mock reproof.

'I was rejected too,' she reminded him, resting her head against his chest. 'You sent me away— told me it was over.'

'I was afraid,' he said. 'Frightened of being hurt—of losing you again when you got tired of playing house.' His mouth twisted. 'Whatever I may have implied, I knew if I took you again it would be for love. And if we made love, it would be forever, on my part anyway.

'But after we'd made love I realised that, however wonderful it had been, there'd been no commitment on your side at all. I'd given you pleasure, but that could be as far as it went. I couldn't take that. I told myself I'd rather be alone for the rest of my life.'

Ross shook his head. 'But, after you left, I felt as if I'd lost half of myself. I knew then that I couldn't let you go. That I'd pay any price to have you with me, even if it only turned out to be for a little while.'

His arms tightened fiercely round her. 'I hope you realise that if you come with me, you'll be giving yourself, heart, body and soul.'

'I know.' She planted a kiss on his chin. 'Will the rest of our lives be long enough?'

'We'll have to see,' he said solemnly. He looked round him, grimacing. 'Get dressed, my love. We're checking out. I'm taking you home.'

'To Trade Winds?'

'Indirectly. *Sweet Bird* is moored there. We're going back to Thunder Cay, to get on with our honeymoon.'

'Then you're not selling it?'

Ross snorted. 'Our own personal paradise? Not a chance. Although I pretended this afternoon that the deal was still on, it was only a ploy to keep you on Fortuna until I could reach you. I was terrified you'd leave—vanish out of my life before I could attempt to make it all right between us.'

He paused. 'But I must admit the shack isn't an ideal bridal suite. And it will never make a family home.'

'Oh, I agree.' Macy thought of the Hilliard house, and the empty rooms where one small tree stretched hopeful branches towards the sky. A living promise of regeneration.

She drew a deep happy breath. 'But I have a dream about that,' she said.

OFFICIAL RULES

FLYAWAY VACATION SWEEPSTAKES 3449

NO PURCHASE OR OBLIGATION NECESSARY

Three Harlequin Reader Service 1995 shipments will contain respectively, coupons for entry into three different prize drawings, one for a trip for two to San Francisco, another for a trip for two to Las Vegas and the third for a trip for two to Orlando, Florida. To enter any drawing using an Entry Coupon, simply complete and mail according to directions.

There is no obligation to continue using the Reader Service to enter and be eligible for any prize drawing. You may also enter any drawing by hand printing the words "Flyaway Vacation," your name and address on a 3"x5" card and the destination of the prize you wish that entry to be considered for (i.e., San Francisco trip, Las Vegas trip or Orlando trip). Send your 3"x5" entries via first-class mail (limit: one entry per envelope) to: Flyaway Vacation Sweepstakes 3449, c/o Prize Destination you wish that entry to be considered for, P.O. Box 1315, Buffalo, NY 14269-1315, USA or P.O. Box 610, Fort Erie, Ontario L2A 5X3, Canada.

To be eligible for the San Francisco trip, entries must be received by 5/30/95; for the Las Vegas trip, 7/30/95; and for the Orlando trip, 9/30/95.

Winners will be determined in random drawings conducted under the supervision of D.L. Blair, Inc., an independent judging organization whose decisions are final, from among all eligible entries received for that drawing. San Francisco trip prize includes round-trip airfare for two, 4-day/3-night weekend accommodations at a first-class hotel, and $500 in cash (trip must be taken between 7/30/95—7/30/96, approximate prize value—$3,500); Las Vegas trip includes round-trip airfare for two, 4-day/3-night weekend accommodations at a first-class hotel, and $500 in cash (trip must be taken between 9/30/95—9/30/96, approximate prize value—$3,500); Orlando trip includes round-trip airfare for two, 4-day/3-night weekend accommodations at a first-class hotel, and $500 in cash (trip must be taken between 11/30/95—11/30/96, approximate prize value—$3,500). All travelers must sign and return a Release of Liability prior to travel. Hotel accommodations and flights are subject to accommodation and schedule availability. Sweepstakes open to residents of the U.S. (except Puerto Rico) and Canada, 18 years of age or older. Employees and immediate family members of Harlequin Enterprises, Ltd., D.L. Blair, Inc., their affiliates, subsidiaries and all other agencies, entities and persons connected with the use, marketing or conduct of this sweepstakes are not eligible. Odds of winning a prize are dependent upon the number of eligible entries received for that drawing. Prize drawing and winner notification for each drawing will occur no later than 15 days after deadline for entry eligibility for that drawing. Limit: one prize to an individual, family or organization. All applicable laws and regulations apply. Sweepstakes offer void wherever prohibited by law. Any litigation within the province of Quebec respecting the conduct and awarding of the prizes in this sweepstakes must be submitted to the Regies des loteries et Courses du Quebec. In order to win a prize, residents of Canada will be required to correctly answer a time-limited arithmetical skill-testing question. Value of prizes are in U.S. currency.

Winners will be obligated to sign and return an Affidavit of Eligibility within 30 days of notification. In the event of noncompliance within this time period, prize may not be awarded. If any prize or prize notification is returned as undeliverable, that prize will not be awarded. By acceptance of a prize, winner consents to use of his/her name, photograph or other likeness for purposes of advertising, trade and promotion on behalf of Harlequin Enterprises, Ltd., without further compensation, unless prohibited by law.

For the names of prizewinners (available after 12/31/95), send a self-addressed, stamped envelope to: Flyaway Vacation Sweepstakes 3449 Winners, P.O. Box 4200, Blair, NE 68009.

RVC KAL